THE REMARKABLE RETURN OF WINSTON POTTER CRISPLY

A NOVEL BY EVE RICE

THE BODLEY HEAD
London . Sydney . Toronto

British Library Cataloguing
in Publication Data
Rice, Eve
The remarkable return of
Winston Potter Crisply.
I. Title
823'.9'1J   PZ7.R3622
ISBN 0-370-30137-4

Printed in Great Britain for
The Bodley Head Ltd
9 Bow Street, London, WC2E 7AL
by Redwood Burn Ltd, Trowbridge
*First published by Greenwillow Books,
William Morrow and Company, Inc., New York 1978*
First published in Great Britain 1978

For Peg and Da—
who make a great team—
with lots and lots of love

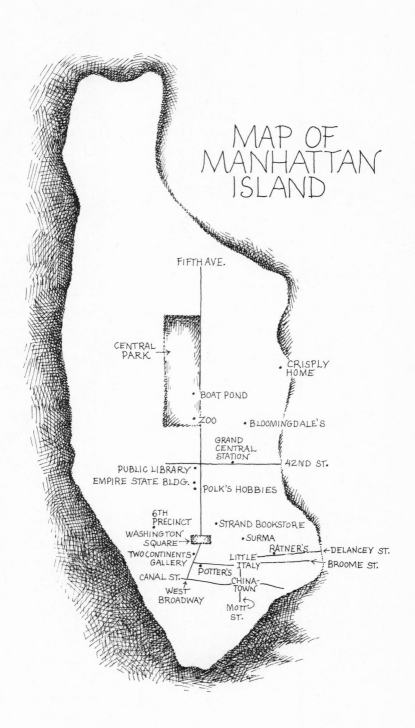

MAP OF
MANHATTAN
ISLAND

FIFTH AVE.

CENTRAL
PARK →

CRISPLY
HOME

• BOAT POND

• ZOO   • BLOOMINGDALE'S

GRAND
CENTRAL
STATION

PUBLIC LIBRARY •   42ND ST.
EMPIRE STATE BLDG. •

• POLK'S HOBBIES

6TH
PRECINCT   • STRAND BOOKSTORE

WASHINGTON   • SURMA
SQUARE →   RATNER'S ← DELANCEY ST.
TWO CONTINENTS •   LITTLE   ← BROOME ST.
GALLERY   ITALY
CANAL ST.   POTTER'S
            WEST   CHINA-
         BROADWAY   TOWN

                        MOTT
                        ST.

THE REMARKABLE RETURN OF
WINSTON POTTER CRISPLY

 1

We would have been on his trail even sooner except that Max has never been a terribly reliable witness— a nice enough little kid, but very impressionable. And I probably wouldn't, had I been given a choice, have picked Max as my partner in this affair—but in the end, everything considered, he did okay.

My lack of choice in the matter was due to the fact that, as Max's older sister and sometime protector, I am responsible for meeting him after school every day and seeing that he gets home safe and sound. As a result of this arrangement, Max and I are together during the most interesting part of the day. Nothing ever happens in school, and little ever happens at home, but after school, out on the streets of New York City is another matter entirely. And it was, of course, after school that it all began.

On that particular day, I picked Max up as usual. Now, my dear little brother is a model-airplane freak who will have to move out of his room pretty soon if he doesn't chuck out some of his early masterpieces. And, as usual, he begged me to take him downtown to Polk's Hobbies for some sort of ultra-neon-metallic paint. Since I was in a pretty good mood, I said yes. So we took the bus down and I guided Max to the glue and paint department at Polk's.

Well, as I said, Max can be the unreliable sort—he's been known to lie as much as any other seven-year-old —so I didn't turn around quickly enough when, in the middle of my reading the poison warning on a can of spray paint, Max suddenly swallowed his gum and gulped, "Potter!"

At first, I thought I'd misunderstood him—but I couldn't think of many other words that sounded like "Potter." And then I thought that Max must be seeing things; but there was poor Max, jumping up and down and pointing and trying not to choke on his gum. Of course, when I looked, there was no one there. Or rather, there was only a bent old saleslady who didn't look a thing like Potter.

"It was Potter! I saw him!"

"You're crazy."

"I am not!"

"Either that, or you're lying."

"I am not lying!" Max looked positively hurt at the suggestion.

"All right, Max, maybe you just need glasses. But you know as well as I do that Potter is in Cambridge —Cambridge, Massachusetts—and even though I realize that your grasp of geography is not terrific, you should be pretty well aware that that's not just around the corner."

Max didn't say anything, so I guess he was willing to accept it as a case of mistaken identity. I went back to amusing myself by reading poison warnings and waited for Max to finish picking out his paints. He's an awful slowpoke on that score, but when it comes to model airplanes, I have to hand it to the kid, he's a real perfectionist.

Max finally found just the right colour (the most poisonous stuff on the shelf) and since the cash register on the second floor was broken, we went downstairs to pay. Just as the cashier was writing up the bill, Max poked me hard. "Potter!"

When I looked, whoever it was had already slipped out the door and was weaving through the crowd on the sidewalk. I had to admit, it did look something like Potter. And if the lady at the register hadn't taken so long about punching in the sale and wrapping up the paint, we could have followed—but she made a regular production out of the whole thing, and by the time she finished, it was far too late.

"Okay, Max," I said. He was gaping at the window. "Let's not jump to any hasty conclusions. We've got to look at this logically. What would Potter be doing in New York when he's supposed to be in Cambridge? And why wouldn't he have told anyone he was here, huh? . . . The obvious answer is that someone who bears a striking resemblance to Potter happens to be running around the city."

Max looked out to the street again and then picked up his bag of paint.

"Yeah," I said. "He's only a look-alike." On the other hand, I was beginning to have my doubts—it's pretty hard to mistake anyone else for your very own flesh-and-blood brother.

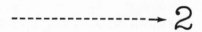 2

I live with a band of eccentrics—my family, that is —but let me start with Potter. Born Winston Potter Crisply, he wisely decided to make the best of that bad situation and picked the most innocuous of his three names; ever after to be called Potter—nothing more and nothing less—by himself, his friends, and his family. Fortunately, both Max and I fared somewhat better in the name game. When it was my turn, my mother and father put their heads together and came up with Rebecca Evangeline Crisply—which is pretty weird but not nearly as bad since it eventually boils down to Rebecca, or Becky for short, which sounds almost normal. And Max, who was brought into this world as Maxwell Bismarck Crisply, could similarly edit his name into acceptability. But poor Potter was stuck. I have always believed that the name someone carries has a lot to do with the kind of person he or she is. I have never known an unpleasant Marsha, for instance, or a happy Eunice. I have never known another Potter, and that is just the point—Potter is one of a kind.

Potter lived in the same large Manhattan brownstone as the rest of us—Mom, Dad, Max, me, our bloodhound, Dan, and our cat, Armenia—until two and a half years ago, which is when he went away to college. Potter is terribly smart. He has the infuriating talent of being able to do just about anything right. He went off to Harvard with a pat on the shoulder from Dad and his flute case under his arm. Future occupation: "the world's most brilliant surgeon"—or, at the very least, "the world's most brilliant doctor." This was family tradition. Potter had announced, at the ripe old age of perhaps six years (I don't remember, as I was too young and I got the story secondhand), "I'm going to be a doctor, just like Daddy." Legend has it that Mom and Dad beamed at each other and then rushed out to get him a doctor's kit with a plastic stethoscope and multicoloured candy pills. Even after finishing the candy pills, Potter still wanted to be a doctor. He dedicated himself to the study of biology, both human and animal. Mom and Dad bought him books; they bought him a microscope. And Potter started eating ants because (he said) they were nutritious, and only gave them up because Mom threatened to stop feeding him anything else if he did not change his ways. He desisted immediately and went back to blueberry blintzes. During the rest of his stay with the family, Potter pulled some pretty strange things out of his bag of tricks, but never anything as disgusting as the ants.

Potter managed to romp through junior high school and then high school and to make things rather tough for me and Max, who were to follow. It is hard for me to explain to my parents why I never come home with report cards that look the way his used to look. I try to remind them that I have other good points. Potter graduated from high school a year early. I gave him a card that said: "Happy graduation and best wishes for all success in your future career as a doctor," after having spent untold hours combing the racks of cards in seventeen stationery stores to find one with just the proper sentiment. For, even though the happy day of his doctorhood was supposedly eight years away (four college, four medical school), I figured I was pretty safe: when Potter sets his mind to something, he *always* does it.

So Potter was off to Harvard. And since then, we have not seen very much of him. He calls regularly, like clockwork, usually to ask Mom or Dad for money. And he writes letters—lots of them. They say that he is studying hard, playing his flute, and looking forward to going to medical school. And meanwhile, back at the brownstone, his childhood toys and first microscope have been packed away and his old room has been turned into a study filled with maps of medieval Europe and scholarly treatises.

Which brings me to another member of our family: my mother. I'd say that everyone in our family age nineteen or older is brilliant. I'd also say that everyone age thirteen or under—which leaves me, Max, Dan, and Armenia—is not. Obviously, my mother is among the brilliant—a fact attested to by the graduate degrees nailed up all over her study wall, and her apparent ease in dealing with the tons of scholarly material she sifts through each week. She is an expert in medieval European history and she teaches a lot. She's home in the mornings to see that Max gets off to school okay (he goes later than I do), but my father is usually home before she is in the evening, as she has some fairly late classes. On Mondays, she doesn't even get home until after Max and I are asleep. She is nice and kind and a good mother. She is also scatterbrained—but she is not nearly as scatterbrained as my father. That is the thing about brilliant people. They do not worry about real life. Real-life worrying is done three times a week by our part-time housekeeper, Rachel, whose comings and goings are hardly noticed at all. But we know that she has been, because things keep on running, and it is an acknowledged fact that without her, everything would stop.

On to my father. As already noted, he is a doctor—a paediatrician, to be exact. He likes kids, even his own. Like my mother, he is nice and kind and he has a study on the opposite side of the hall from hers. He reads medical journals incessantly and writes articles too, and often, the rat-tap-tapping of his typing is echoed across the hall as my mother pounds away with equal vigour on her matching Smith Corona. They have the perfect marriage. They love to listen to each other work.

My father is also a numismatist—that is, he collects coins, mostly old ones. His hobby is the one source of tension in our household, as my mother cannot understand how a man who cares so much about old money does not care enough about new money to balance his chequebook. But over the years, my father seems to have become inured to any protest.

Anyway, at this point in the family catalogue, the personnel becomes rather boring. Max is too young to be of much interest. If he lives up to the general level of his past performance, perfection in model airplanes notwithstanding, he will probably not be brilliant. He is just normal, like me. For a little brother, he is okay. He does not steal my things more than is absolutely necessary. He does not cry a lot, nor pout, nor scratch, nor bite.

Then there is Dan, who is a very floppy dog. He is affectionate—if you like that sort of thing. And there is Armenia, who is just a cat. Oh, and of course, there is me: thirteen-year survivor in a den of neurotics; a decent student; a hardworking, loyal sister; and at the point that I left my story, soon to become an amateur detective.

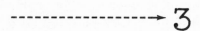 **3**

After the incident in Polk's Hobbies, both Max and I temporarily forgot about the appearance of Potter—or Potter's look-alike. I three-quarters believed that it was his double. But I soon changed my mind.

A week and a half later, I picked Max up after school, per usual.

"Beck, how about going over to the park?"

I thought about it for a minute. One of the nice things about having two working parents and being at a trustworthy age is that no one is waiting for you to walk in the door at three o'clock—you don't even have to telephone.

"Sure. I don't have much homework anyway. Lead on."

So Max led, exactly where I thought he would lead— straight to the zoo. Max has a thing about zoos. I think he identifies with the animals.

He immediately raced over to the tall, round monkey cages. He laughed. The monkeys laughed. He scratched. The monkeys scratched. And then he grabbed my arm.

"Potter!" He pointed. The monkeys pointed too.

Squinting through the monkey bars, I could see that he was looking at a dark, cloaked figure on the other side of the seal pool. And this time I could see that Max was right. No doubt about it—it *was* Potter. He was standing with a pad in his hand and appeared to be jotting down some sort of notes.

I nodded and Max started to tear off after him. I had only nodded to indicate my agreement, but unfortunately, Max mistook my nod for "attack"—so, sorry to say, I had to trip him. One nice thing about Max is that he is not very breakable.

"For crying out loud! Why'd you do that?"

"Silly! You can't just rush off after him. He's supposed to be in Cambridge. Maybe he doesn't want us to know he's here. We have to proceed with caution."

Max was trying to pick the pebbles out of the knees of his blue jeans.

"Right?"

"Right, what?" Max said.

"We have to go slowly, Max. You're too impetuous."

"I don't know what that means."

"Forget it. We've just got to be a little more subtle, that's all. First we watch. Then we move."

Potter was beginning to pace in front of the seals. He closed up his pad, put it under his arm, and walked up the steps.

"All right. Come on. Slowly."

Max and I followed a good way behind, crouching below the hedge, and proceeded in this manner until Potter walked through a door. As luck would have it, it was the men's room. Well, I certainly wasn't going to follow him in there. Anyway, even Max couldn't go in because Potter surely would have seen him. So we positioned ourselves behind two columns that were conveniently situated for keeping an eye on the door and waited—and waited and waited.

"Max. Psssst, Max!"

"What?"

"Either he's drowned or there are two doors to the

men's room and we've been watching the wrong one. You'll have to go and see."

Max furrowed his brow, put his jacket collar up, and, after carefully looking both ways, dashed to the door and pushed it open. Then he disappeared.

A few minutes later, someone tapped me on the shoulder from behind.

"You were right," Max said. "There are two doors."

And that is how we lost Potter a second time.

 4

Seeing as Max had been a pretty good kid all afternoon, I decided to treat him, and me, to a soft ice-cream cone. Soft ice cream is soft ice cream, but this stuff was bordering on soup. It was pretty difficult to do any serious talking in between licks—but I tried.

"You know, Max, I'll bet Mom and Dad don't know Potter's in New York either. And if the person we saw at Polk's really was Potter, then he's made two secret trips to the city in the last two weeks—or else he's been here for two weeks straight. Which is pretty strange, considering that it's the middle of the term and the middle of the week—and seems at least to suggest the possibility that he is up to something rotten, yes?" I tried to plug up the leak in the bottom of my cone, but to no avail. "Of course, there may be an innocent explanation for the whole thing—but I'll give you ten-to-one odds against it." I licked the soft ice cream off my fingers. "What do you think?"

Max, who has never been loquacious, phrased his answer succinctly. "I think I'd like another ice-cream cone."

I don't begrudge the kid his ice-cream cones. It's just that, as a result of my tender heart and Max's enormous appetite, we had to walk home. I didn't realize it at the time, but the two quarters I handed Max were an integral part of our bus fare. After that, I had only enough for one ride and I am not a nasty enough person to have taken the bus myself and let Max walk. On the other hand, I am not a nice enough person to have let Max take the bus without me. So we trudged home together. Max clung to me with one hand and dragged his book bag along the sidewalk with the other. This is Max's favourite posture—it makes him look like an airplane banking for a turn. It is also primarily responsible for his destruction of three book bags in the same school year.

When we opened the front door, I could hear my mother's cheery voice in the living room.

"Oh, there you are, Becky. Is Max with you?" (Do not mistake this last for parental concern; it was merely curiosity.)

"Yes, Mom."

"I'm on the phone. I'm talking to your brother."

"Potter? Where is he?"

"Cambridge, dear. Of course. Would you like to say hello?"

I looked at Max, who whispered, "Maybe he flew back?" Exactly what I would have expected from a model airplane freak with no sense of time or geography. Tired as I was, I raced to the phone.

"Potter?"

"Hi, kid."

"Hi, how are you?"

"Oh, fine. I'm studying hard, playing my flute, and looking forward to going to medical school."

Very subtle now. "How's Cambridge—how's the weather?"

"Not bad. I went jogging along the Charles this afternoon."

"Yeah, I'll bet," I said and turned the phone back over to my mother.

Max was stuffing his book bag under the bench in the hall.

"Gee, he sure got back to Cambridge quick."

"Max, Potter is not in Cambridge. It would be impossible."

"Rockets?" suggested Max.

I felt it was best to ignore the comment and leave his impressionable young mind to the care of his teachers. "He must have called from a pay phone somewhere in New York—and he is *purposely* misleading us. It's very suspicious, very suspicious indeed." Then something else occurred to me. "Max, we obviously can't mention anything about this to Mom or Dad—we don't want to get Potter into trouble until we know for sure how rotten this rotten thing he's up to is. You understand?"

Max kicked his bag a few times, hoping to permanently wedge it against the wall. "I won't tell," Max said and then added, "if we can be partners."

"Partners?"

"I get to help look for Potter."

"What makes you think I'm going to go off looking for him?"

"I would," said Max.

And he was right, I would too. "All right. Partners. But this is all hush-hush."

"Okay. Hush-hush," Max said and gave his book bag a final, savage kick.

----------------→ 5

"Max! Rebecca! Wash up. We're having dinner in a few minutes."

By the time I got to the downstairs bathroom, Max was already creating elaborate designs on the white guest towels with his supposedly clean hands.

"Max, don't you ever use soap?"

"Of course, I do," said Max.

Actually, there was no need to have asked such a silly question—one look at the soap dish should have been sufficient. I gingerly picked up the dirt-encrusted bar and began to wash my hands. Max stood in the door.

"Where do you think Potter is now?" he asked.

"A hotel, a friend's—I don't know."

"How are we going to find out?"

The sixty-four-thousand-dollar question.

"Well, we've only got a city of eight million people to sort through."

"Seven million, eight hundred ninety-five thousand, five hundred and sixty-three," corrected Max. "As of 1970."

"Thanks." I grabbed a clean towel before Max could hand it to me. "What we do know is that Potter has been to the zoo, and probably Polk's Hobbies, as well.

But that's precious little to go on."

"We could try the zoo again," Max said. "Maybe he'll come back?"

"Congratulations. Exactly what I was thinking. It's a fairly slim chance—but it's all we've got. So, as of to-morrow, we will stake out the zoo. It's Saturday. We'll start early and spend the day."

"Oh, goodie!" said Max and began scratching himself and making noises like a monkey.

I was beginning to suspect that Max was more inter-ested in continuing a dialogue with his animal cronies than in finding his lost brother; still, it was comforting to think that we were about to undertake some pur-poseful action.

 6

At least, that was the plan before my father dropped his bombshell at dinner. It was right after Max had mashed all his peas to a fine consistency and sculpted them into a carefully rounded mound, and right before he swirled the ketchup into his mashed potatoes.

"Max, not at the table," said my mother.

"Where else am I supposed to do it?" Bright kid.

"To think that a child so carefully—and lovingly—

reared by his devoted parents should have such abominable table manners," mused my father. "I hope you can refrain from such artistic excesses over the weekend —Uncle Arthur and Aunt Emily are very squeamish."

I managed to swallow the lump of mashed potatoes that had caught in my throat. "Uncle Arthur?"

"Sure," said my mother as she grabbed the ketchup bottle. "You remember. We told you we were going up there for the weekend. It will do all of us city slickers good to get out to the country for some fresh air and a rest."

"I just want to catch up on the *New England Journal of Medicine*," said my father.

"Do we have to?" I asked. "Please, can't we stay home?"

"Oh, come on. Allen and Frannie may be your cousins, but they're not all *that* bad. Just think what they're probably saying about you—'Aw, do we have to? Becky and Max are no fun at all.'" My father's falsetto was unbecoming.

"It's not Allen and Frannie I mind. That was last year. It's just that I have a lot of things I want to do in the city—I was even going to take Max to the zoo."

"Ah," said my mother, "now we know where he gets his table manners. It's just as well that you don't."

I looked at Mom. Then at Dad. The case was obviously settled. And things appeared to be working out very badly. Not only did Potter not want to be found, but Fate seemed to be protecting him from us as well.

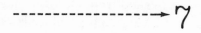 7

You can probably guess what kind of a weekend it was. Frustrating. I really don't hate my cousins any more; but they are not the sort of people to be bogged down with when you are in the middle of something important.

Actually, under other circumstances, it would have been a very pleasant weekend. The weather was warm and sunny. My parents spent their time cooing at every crocus and daffodil they saw. Cousin Allen had a new tri-coloured Frisbee that whistled. Max was the model of charm-school etiquette at table and otherwise. And Frannie, who has stopped sticking her gum behind her ear, had taken down all her pictures of Donny Osmond. The Scotch-tape marks on the wall were a definite improvement. For two days, we mostly ate and slept, and in between, Uncle Arthur and Aunt Emily entertained us with duets for glockenspiel and double bass. It could have been worse. Meanwhile, I was busy counting the minutes until we headed for home.

We didn't get back until 9:00 P.M. on Sunday. Mom and Dad stowed their tennis rackets and put the bouquet of budding forsythia on the coffee table in the living room.

My father, rosy-cheeked from all his cooing and resting, said, "Now, that wasn't such a bad weekend, was it?"

"Lovely," said my mother.

I figured they could argue that one out by themselves, and disappeared. When I walked into Max's room, he was already in bed, curled around his teddy bear, waiting for Mom and Dad to come and say good night.

"Well, Max," I said. "Looks like we'll be able to start tomorrow after school."

"Oh, good!" Even in the semidarkness, I could see Max's eyes sparkle.

"Beck?"

"Yeah?"

"Would you turn on my night light?"

"Great. I have a partner who sleeps with a teddy bear *and* a night light."

"And, Beck?"

"Yes, Watson?"

"I've been thinking—how do we know that Potter hasn't gone back to Cambridge by now?"

"Max," I said. "Stop thinking."

-----------------→ 8

Fate, having made no secret of whose side it was on, struck again on Monday morning. Ergo, I woke up with an awful sore throat.

"Good morning," my mother said as I walked into the kitchen.

"Good morning," I croaked in return.

"Oh, dear. You sound awful. What's the matter?"

"Nothing," I said. "May I have some oatmeal?"

"Open your mouth. Let me see."

My mother made me stick out my tongue and say "Ahhhhh." Of course, it wouldn't have occurred to her to get a professional medical opinion from the gentleman who was just then on his way out the front door.

She stopped, though, in mid-squint to call after him. "Good-bye, Honey. Don't forget tonight's my late night. I think Becky's sick."

"I'll be home early-ish," said my father. "Good-bye." And he slammed the door.

"Now, let me see," my mother said, turning to me again. I knew as well as she did that she couldn't see a thing in that light.

"It does *not* look good. Stay home from school today."

"Aw, Mom. I'm okay. Really."

"No, I don't want it to get worse. It could lead to something—bronchitis, or even pneumonia." No one would ever have believed that this woman was married to a doctor.

"You can go back tomorrow if you feel okay."

"Please?"

"Absolutely not."

When my mother makes up her mind, it is simply no use. She set about making my oatmeal with great zeal, undoubtedly delighted with one of her rare opportunities to play Clara Barton—at least for the hour and a half before she set off to work. There is nothing like disease to let a working mother show how much she cares.

I sat at the table alternately decorating my oatmeal with brown sugar and then skimming the good part off the top, until Max appeared.

"Oatmeal?" asked Mom cheerily.

"Okay," Max said, and then to me, "Why are you still in your pyjamas? You're supposed to be gone."

"I'm sick," I said.

"You don't look sick."

I glared at him. "Mother *says* I'm sick."

"Oh." Max understood. "Does that mean we can't go to the zoo?"

"You guessed it." I lowered my voice. "I'd sneak out, but Mom told Dad I was sick and I don't know how early he'll be home."

"Gee," said Max. "We'll never find Potter."

"You may have a point there." Just then, the phone rang.

"Hello? Oh, Potter! Hello!" Mother chirped as she gesticulated with the wooden spoon she had been using to stir Max's oatmeal. "Oh, yes. Yes, of course. No. Not at all. How was your weekend? We went to Arthur and Emily's. Yes, all of us. . . ." Listening to one side of a telephone conversation is nothing more than a lesson in futility.

I waited until she had replaced the receiver and then asked as casually as I could, "What was that all about?"

"The usual. Your brother is studying hard, etcetera. And he's broke and needs money." She gave the second batch of oatmeal a final stir and poured it into Max's bowl. Then she sat down and took out her chequebook. "That boy certainly does go through a lot of money. I can't imagine what he does with it all. Oh, well. . . ." She signed the cheque with a flourish, slipped it into an envelope, and placed it on her brief case. "I'm going to get dressed." She stopped to pick up the sugar box and eyed it critically. "And, Becky, make sure Max has a little oatmeal with his brown sugar, will you?" With that, she left the room.

----------------→ 9

I had just comfortably settled myself on the living-
room sofa and was in the process of reading a really
super book, when Rachel walked in.

"Goodness! What are you doing here?"

"I'm sick."

Rachel looked at me carefully. I could see that she
was holding her breath.

"It's all right. It's not contagious."

She let out a sigh.

"Actually," she said, "you don't look sick."

"Actually," I said, "I'm not. I had a sore throat this
morning, but I think it must have been from sleeping
with my mouth open or something."

"Oh, I see," she said. "Nope. You don't look sick at
all. And in that case, would you mind moving? I thought
I'd start on the living room."

Rachel is no pushover.

Ordinarily, I would have enjoyed being sick, but
being confined to quarters when there is urgent business
to attend to greatly diminishes the pleasure. I was glad
when Max was finally delivered to the door by one of his

teachers at three o'clock. My father arrived at six.

"Hello, kids." He put his briefcase down and lit his pipe. "And how's the patient?"

"Fine. I'm not sick."

"Glad to hear it," said my father. He peered at me closely. "Open your mouth."

I did.

"Oho! One exquisite set of teeth, one tongue, and—not much else." He straightened up. "I pronounce you cured. And now," he said, "what would you kids like for dinner?"

This usually meant a choice of Campbell's Soup or Campbell's Soup.

"No opinions? Very well, it will be a surprise."

It was not. It was Campbell's chicken noodle soup with grilled cheese sandwiches. The only surprise was that Max and I got to do the dishes—usually my father and I do them.

"Max, old boy, you are growing up. Just hold on tight, don't drop anything, and everything will be okay." With that, my father handed Max a dish towel.

A moment later, the phone rang. Dad's first words were enough to make *me* almost drop a dish.

"Hello, Potter! How are you. Hmmmm. Yes. It can be arranged. No. No. Not at all. . . ." I strained to hear, but as usual, the half conversation was meaningless.

My father finally finished the call and turned around. "Max, I presume the dishes are dry, because nothing else is."

Max looked hurt.

"What did Potter want?" I said and rinsed the last dish.

"Your brother? The usual. He is studying hard, playing his flute, looking forward to going to medical school —and he's broke and wants money. Very normal American kid."

My father got his chequebook and wrote out a cheque for Potter, signed it, and deposited it in an envelope. "I'm retreating to my study if anybody needs me."

"That's *awfully* strange," I said to Max as I sponged off the floor.

"It's not so strange. He always works in his study."

"Not Dad. Potter. Calling for money twice in one day." I moved over to mop under the refrigerator. "Wait a minute! Potter knows Mom works late on Monday nights; he knows Dad leaves earlier in the morning. And he called once when each of them was home alone. Since they don't see each other all day, the chances are pretty good that they'll forget to mention the calls to each other—and so each of them will think he's the only one writing Potter a cheque. What a racket!"

"He does it all the time," said Max.

I whirled around. "What do you mean, 'he does it all the time'?"

"Potter calls twice every Monday. Didn't you know?"

"How could I? I've never been sick on a Monday before." I crossed my arms and said in my best big-sister voice, "Max, didn't these double calls ever strike you as being a little odd?"

"No."

To my little brother's generally excellent sense of time and geography, I now felt it necessary to add his ability to reason in financial matters.

"How long has Potter been doing this?"

Max cocked his head to one side. "I don't know. Forever?"

"Could you be a little more specific?"

"Since September—maybe. I don't remember exactly."

"I don't get it. I just don't get it. Why does Potter need so much money? Even if he does take an occasional jaunt to New York, it's not *that* expensive. And all the other stuff is cared for by his college room and board fee—food, clean sheets, a place to sleep, everything. All his living expenses in Cambridge are paid, unless . . . ."

I looked Max straight in the eye. "Max, my dear, this situation is far more interesting than even we originally suspected."

"But, Becky, I don't understand," Max stage-whispered as I closed the kitchen door and positioned him as a sentry.

"I'll explain it in a minute. But for now, just make sure that Dad doesn't walk in while I'm calling Potter."

"Why should he care if we call Potter?"

"Well, first, it's long distance. And second, it just might look a little suspicious; you and I don't exactly call Potter every day."

"Oh." Max put his ear to the door and listened with the serious concentration of a true professional.

I called the number in Boston which my mother had listed in her special book.

Two rings. Click.

"Hello?"

"Hello. May I speak with Potter Crisply, please? This is his sister."

"Potter? Oh, wow. Potter. Sure. Well, he's not here right now. Can I have him call you back?"

"When will he be in?"

"Oh, uh, he didn't say. But I can have him call you if you want me to."

"No, that's okay. It's not important."

"Sure?"

"Yeah. You don't even have to tell him that I called."

"Okay."

"Thanks. Good-bye."

Click. Click.

"Just as I thought—what a setup." Max was still glued to the door. "It's all right, Max. You can relax now."

Max slumped onto the kitchen floor. "I'm relaxed. Now will you tell me what's going on?"

"Sure. It's very simple. Potter's not visiting New York, he's living here—I'm almost positive. It would account for his needing so much money and it would explain some other things which have been bothering me as well. Have you ever noticed how often—apart from the Monday business—he calls home?"

"An awful lot."

"Right—entirely *too* often for any red-blooded, self-respecting, all-American kid. It's as though he were calling Mom and Dad so they wouldn't call him. Because, if they did call Cambridge, I'll bet they'd find he was out—always. But to make doubly sure they don't figure it out, he's conned his roommate into covering for him."

"Covering?"

"Covering up. If someone calls, his roommate says, 'I'll have him call you back when he gets in'—the same thing he told me a minute ago. Then his roommate calls him in New York and Potter calls the person back from a New York phone, but the person *thinks* he's calling from Cambridge. Nice, huh?"

"Hmmmm," said Max. He was biting his lip in concentration. "Does he do that with letters too?"

"Good thinking, Max. That's our next stop. I think we may find some interesting information in that department too."

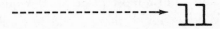 11

"Where are we going?" Max asked as I dragged him down the hall.

"To Mom and Dad's bedroom—to see if we can find Potter's old letters."

I took a quick peek into my father's study and was relieved to see that he was still absorbed in some fascinating medical literature. We were doing very well until Max slipped on the stairs. He sounded rather like a ton of bricks (strange for a fifty-five-pound weakling) being dropped from a great height. Max whimpered.

I took his arm. "Shhh. I know you can only fall down noisily but try to pick yourself up quietly. Are you hurt?"

Unbreakable Max sniffled. "No, I'm okay."

I held my breath, waiting for my father to appear, but only sleepy old Dan shuffled out from underneath the stairs.

"Come on, Max. But be more careful."

"I *was* being careful," he said indignantly, "I just fell, that's all."

My parents are inveterate packrats—and the closet behind their bed is a convenient storage hole. A little exploration uncovered rolls and rolls of Max's nursery-school finger paintings; a little more exploration produced a box of Potter's letters, all written within the past year. I pulled out a stack and undid the rubber band.

"So we're looking for New York postmarks?" asked Max.

"Right—he probably figured no one would notice, even though they were supposedly mailed from Cambridge."

Wrong. I sorted through the envelopes. Cambridge. Cambridge. Cambridge. All of them. "How disappointing!"

Then I began to read through the letters; they all said the same old thing. However, a minute later, something caught my eye and I spread them all out. "There's nothing much in what he writes, but look at the *way* he writes it!"

Max looked and shook his head. "They haven't taught me to read script in school yet." So much for a liberal education.

"That, my dear, is beside the point—even a non-reader should be able to see *something*. These letters for October are all written in black ink. Yes?"

"So?"

"And November's are all green. And December's are in blue. Definite pattern. Too consistent."

"Huh?"

"If your typical college student had written these letters, he would have used the different coloured pens at random—but these groups of letters are so neatly arranged. A month a colour. A month a pen."

"Why would Potter do it like that?"

"Well, it leads me to suspect that Potter wrote each group of letters at the beginning of each month, all at the same time—which is a pretty peculiar way for a normal person to write letters. On the other hand, it wouldn't be odd at all—just convenient and cheap—if he had to send the whole bunch back to Cambridge so that they could be re-mailed separately and stamped with a Cambridge postmark. I'd say that Potter has a very well-trained roommate. Or rather, I should say, *accomplice*."

"Wow," said Max. "You're smart. I never would have figured that out."

"Elementary, my dear. Elementary." I noticed that Max had unrolled some of his old finger paintings and was now gazing lovingly at his own work. It was obviously time to move. "Come on. We've got one more thing to check into tonight," I said and stood up.

"Where are we going?"

"Downstairs—if you think you can make it."

"Of course, I can," said Max disdainfully and followed me into the hall.

 12

Max took the stairs as carefully as if he had just learned to walk, without making a sound—which was a good thing, considering that this next part was going to be pretty tricky. Although my parents kept letters and other ultimately expendable collections in the aforementioned packrat storage, all the really important documents were carefully put away in the official file downstairs, which file happened to be in my mother's study, and which study just happened to be across the hall from the room in which my father was working— a fact of some importance, since I was well aware that as far as Max and I were concerned, the file had been declared off limits.

I peeked in at my father as we passed. He was hunched over his desk, squinting, with his glasses pushed back on his head, pipe in one hand and pen in the other, writing furiously. From his enthusiasm, one might easily have assumed him to be triumphantly formulating a cure for the common cold, but a quick look revealed that he was only doing the *New York Times* crossword puzzle. Max and I tiptoed past, into my mother's study. ·

The file cabinet in question was an old, secondhand affair—the squeaky kind. But at least it was not locked. I pulled a drawer open slowly, which only exacerbated its tendency to groan. Dan, with his finely tuned sense of hearing, came padding round the corner.

"Wrong drawer." I closed it carefully and opened the one below. Dan whimpered.

"Shhh! Max, hold Dan. He's drooling on everything." Max threw his arms around Dan's neck and they both gazed in silent anticipation. I reached for the folder marked "S." School. School reports.

"Aha!" I said as I pulled out Potter's grades and looked through them. "Max, this clinches it!" I held the papers up. Dan sniffed at them briefly and then left the room in disgust.

"They look pretty good to me," said Max. "All A's and B's. Potter sure is smart."

"That's just it. All A's *and* B's. Never, never in all his

life has Potter come home with less than an A. Here, look. His first two years at Harvard, he gets all A's. But this year, there are B's—lots of them."

"Maybe he got tired?"

"Not Potter. Potter is indefatigable."

"Inde- what?"

"Tireless, Max. Tireless."

"Oh. . . . Then what?"

"Don't you see? It all fits. If Potter isn't living in Cambridge, then he's not going to his classes either. Which means that someone else is using his name and going to classes for him—someone who is not as brilliant as Potter—and it is that other person's grades which are being sent home."

"Wow," said Max.

"Yup. It's the last detail in a perfect hoax calculated to have us all believe that Potter is a student at Harvard —when, in fact, he is nothing of the kind."

 13

Max picked up the folder to replace Potter's grades, but as a result of his deft handling, everything else spilled out.

"Max." I sighed.

"I'm sorry, but it slipped."

We started to pick up the scattered items, but in the middle of doing so, Max started to laugh. "Look at these pictures of Potter."

They were the typical high-school stuff—mostly. A number were stuck together with something that looked like dried-out jam. Max passed one to me. "Potter sure looks funny in that one."

I had to admit that it was not the most dignified picture I had ever seen. Potter stood smiling, with blue stains on his white T-shirt and bluish smudges all over his face. It was comforting to note that Potter had not always had *everything* under control.

"Blueberry blintzes," I said and piled the rest of the photographs and papers together. "Here, give me the folder."

"Blueberry blintzes?"

"Blueberry blintzes. Blueberry blintzes!" I grabbed Max by the shoulders. "Old buddy, we are *not* going to the zoo tomorrow!"

"But, Becky, you said . . . ."

"Shhh. I've got a better idea. Listen. Now, tell me, what do you know about Potter's eating habits?"

"Not much."

"Well, the most obvious thing is that he eats incessantly—he's tall and skinny and he's got the metabolism of a shrew."

36

"So?"

"So," —my reasoning was brilliant, even if I do say so myself—"what's his favourite food in all the world?"

"Blueberry blintzes?"

"And where, according to one Winston Potter Crisply, do they make the best blueberry blintzes in all of New York City? Where, on the days that he had both the time and the money, could one formerly have found the said Mr. Crisply enjoying an after-school snack?"

"Um . . . uh. . . ."

"Ratner's, my dear Max, of course! So tomorrow we will begin our search at Ratner's."

Max regarded me with appropriate awe.

"But right now, we've got to get all this stuff put back," I said and shoved the pictures and the grades into the folder and jammed the whole thing into the file somewhere in the vicinity of "S." The click of the file drawer closing coincided with the slam of the front door.

My father, Dan, and Armenia, all summoned by the noise, preceded us into the front hall.

"Ah. Lovely to see how well the house functions in my absence," my mother said and pointed an accusing finger at us. "Why aren't you in bed?"

My father took my mother's coat and kissed her. "Sorry. It's my fault. I forgot all about them." The true confessions of a dedicated parent.

"Likely story. Oh, well. You two get washed and

we'll be up in a minute to say good night." Thankful for our dismissal, Max and I scrambled up the stairs and into bed.

 14

When I arrived to pick up Max the next afternoon, he was already outside, contentedly destroying his new shoes by kicking his heels against the brick wall on which he was perched.

"Ready?" asked Max.

"Ready—almost. Come on." I started walking.

"Well, you're going the wrong way. The subway is that way."

"I'm well aware, thank you, but I thought, in the interests of efficiency, that we might drop our things off at home. I refuse to drag you *and* your book bag all over town. Besides, I remembered something."

"What?" Max jumped down from the wall in such a way as to scuff the toes of his shoes as well. Quite a feat.

"The one point we overlooked is that we can't watch Potter if he can watch us. Or, to put it another way, since he obviously wants to remain incognito, we had better travel incognito too."

Max looked puzzled.

"What we need, Max, is a disguise!"

"Oh! Oh, goodie! What kind?"

"Versatile, utilitarian, and not too conspicuous."

Max thought hard. "I've got my Superman costume from last Halloween."

"Well, I had something a little less flashy in mind. But we'll see. I'm sure we'll find something."

Max actually proved to be no problem at all in that regard.

"Put on these jeans."

"But Mom says I can't wear them out of the house. They've got holes."

"I won't tell, I promise." I rumpled Max's hair and smeared a little of my mother's charcoal eyebrow pencil under his eyes. I thought about giving him a moustache too but decided that he looked a trifle young to be sprouting facial hair. I settled for a bit of rouge on his cheeks.

"And this shirt." It was red-checked and too big. "And tie." Vile combination.

"Tie?"

"Yes, tie. Seven-year-olds hardly ever wear ties. It's a good touch. Here, your jacket is ratty enough the way it is. But keep the collar up. And the hat—very important item. You must keep it pulled down close to your eyes. There."

"How do I look?"

"Even your own mother wouldn't know you."

"You mean brother, I hope," said Max. "What about you?"

"Follow me."

I found the long skirt from my old gypsy costume in the closet, courtesy of last year's school musical, and took a white blouse which was hanging nearby. Then the bandana, the earrings, a good measure of lipstick, and a little something to darken my eyes.

"Oh, and these. The final touch."

"White tennis sneakers?"

"My dear Max, everybody has to walk." I tied them on—with double knots. "How do I look?"

"Like a gypsy with white tennis sneakers."

I smoothed my skirt and looked in the mirror. "Hmmmm. Not bad. Come along," and we hurried downstairs, stopping only long enough for me to grab my goose-down parka from the hall closet. Then, ready at last, I followed Max out the front door and down the steps—remembering only after the latch had clicked that I had forgotten to take my keys.

---------------→ 15

We emerged from the subway somewhere in the vicinity of Lafayette Street to find ourselves serenaded by the clank of hammers, the rumble of trucks, and the whine of drills.

Max tried to shout above the noise. "Becky, are you sure you know the way?"

"I'm absolutely one-hundred-percent sure," I said, in spite of the fact that I'd only been to Ratner's once before and was not very sure at all—but I hoped we would arrive before Max had a chance to learn the truth. For once, luck was with me and we were soon marching along Delancey Street, whose sidewalks were swarming with people.

"Don't get lost, Max," I cautioned—unnecessarily, since he had already dug his fingernails securely into my palm. And although I have an exceptionally high tolerance for pain, I was rather glad when we finally left the bustle and din of the street and slipped into the calm interior of Ratner's Dairy Restaurant.

"Wow, this is a big place," Max said as he let go of my hand and gazed around at a room filled with shiny formica tables, arranged in four neat, military rows.

Canned music emanated from every inch of the pink ceiling. The restaurant was not terribly busy at that hour—apparently not an "in" place with the after-school crowd.

A man in a business suit approached us. He eyed us coldly. "What can I do for you?"

"We'd like a table."

"Are you sure?" He looked unhappy.

"Yes."

"Absolutely?"

"Yes. I'm absolutely sure," I said and then sotto voce to Max, "What kind of a way is this to run a business?"

"Look in the mirror," he whispered back.

I caught a glimpse of us in the mirrors that panelled the left-hand side of the room. "The man's right—I wouldn't seat us either." Going incognito does have its drawbacks. However, there was no need to ask specially for a dark, out-of-the-way table—one that would be good for seeing and not being seen—as the man immediately steered us to the darkest corner in the place.

"Stop!" I ordered Max as he started to take off his jacket. "That's part of your disguise. And keep the collar up."

"I've got to take off my hat, Becky. Mom always says . . . ."

"Forget the etiquette, Max. Etiquette and important business do not mix."

We both sat down facing the door and the street, where a huge plate-glass window allowed the afternoon sun to stream in on the fake flowers. "What now?" he asked.

"Well, we've got to order something. They won't let us sit here unless we do."

"That's okay with me, I'm hungry." Good old dependable Max. "Where's the waiter?"

I looked around. A grey-haired waiter in a yellow jacket and black bow tie was fiddling with the napkins on a nearby table, doing his best to postpone our inevitable meeting.

"Ahemmm," I cleared my throat. "Ahemmm." And tapped my spoon casually on my water glass.

He frowned, refolded the napkin twice, and slowly ambled over. "Yes?"

"May we see a menu, please?" I pronounced the words as precisely as I could so that he would know we had been well brought up in spite of our dubious appearance.

"Of course," he said and bowed slightly. With a flick of his wrist, he produced two menus, seemingly out of thin air. Then he retreated.

I looked at the menu and gulped. "Uh-oh, here goes this week's allowance. Maybe we can just order one thing."

"For you or for me?" asked Max. The way he asked

the question was an answer in itself.

"For you, Max. I'm not really hungry. Besides, don't forget that we're here on business."

"Right," said Max.

Our waiter re-materialized. "Yes? What will it be?"

"What will you have, Max?"

He fingered the edge of the menu. "I don't see it here, but may I have a hamburger?"

The waiter's eyebrows rose in astonishment. *"This,"* he said, "is a dairy restaurant, and *that's* not kosher!" He stormed off.

"Ooops," I said.

"Kosher?" asked Max. "What did I say?"

"Well, dear, if I remember correctly, your food request violates Jewish dietary law."

"You're kidding."

"No, really. If someone's kosher, then he doesn't eat things like meat and dairy products together—not on the same plate, not with the same silverware, nothing. And if this is a kosher dairy restaurant, then they don't even serve meat." I surveyed the menu quickly to make sure that this was indeed the case. It was.

"Choose something else."

"What? All they've got is stuff I can't pronounce."

"Try the blueberry blintzes. They'll bring us luck." I was about to clear my throat again for attention when the waiter returned. He had calmed down considerably.

"Have you settled on your order?"

"Yes," Max said, "I will have the blueberry blintzes."

"And?"

"And two forks," I said. The waiter raised both eyebrows. Then he grabbed the menus, turned quickly on his heel, and hurried off.

"Maybe," said Max, "that's not kosher either."

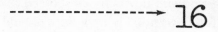 **16**

Unfortunately, there was still no sign of Potter. I looked at the front door and at the crowds rushing by on the sidewalk outside, and then at the people scattered here and there throughout the restaurant.

"I hope he comes," said Max, reading my thoughts.

"I do too. But be patient. We've got to be patient."

Max's idea of being patient was making silly faces at himself in the mirrors, which were now on our right. It was the perfect table for an egomaniac.

"Your blintzes will be here in a minute, sir," said our waiter and slapped down a plastic basket of rolls and a butter dish. He returned almost immediately with a large plate and set it down before Max. Three huge, crisp dough envelopes lay there, oozing blueberry syrup from their corners. And separately, on a round dish, sat a pristine lump of sour cream.

"Well, dig in," I said.

Max was about to launch himself at the blintzes but I steadied his hand. "But slowly," I said. "They have to last us awhile because when they're gone, we'll have to leave." I looked to the front again. Nothing.

Max, a born gourmet, smeared a little sour cream on his blintzes and took a bite.

"Hot!" he said and hurriedly swallowed the mouthful, which was followed quickly by a dose of cold water. He cut another bite, blew on it carefully, and then proceeded with caution.

"Not bad. Try some." He shoved the plate at me.

"Not good," I said. "Here," and shoved it back. I looked at the door again and then settled down to watch iron-stomached Max eat the blueberries out of his blintzes, one by one—an appropriately time-consuming process, and one that afforded me the leisure to wonder if perhaps we had made a mistake in not returning to the zoo. We waited.

Long about the two-thousandth blueberry, however, our patience was finally rewarded. I almost gave Max an instant tonsillectomy by grabbing his arm.

"It's Potter!"

Max quickly disengaged himself from me and the fork.

A tall, slim figure, dressed in a long, dark cape and a wide-brimmed hat, made his way through the front door, past the bakery counter, and up to the man in the suit, who then led him to a table two rows over and three spaces up from the one at which we sat. As he removed his hat, any lingering doubt about his being Potter quickly vanished.

"Why does he dress like that?" Max asked. "He looks like a spy or something."

"Just eccentric," I said. "You know."

Potter looked around. He looked at us. Max quickly speared another blueberry. I pretended to be absorbed in examining the salt shaker. "I think he knows we're watching him," Max whispered.

Potter's waiter returned. "Yes, sir?"

"I'll have the blueberry blintzes, please. And coffee." The waiter bowed and left. Potter unfolded his napkin and then looked at us again. I turned my head to the wall. Of course!

"Max! The mirrors!" How convenient. All Max and I had to do was to glance nonchalantly down the length of the room and a little to the right, and Potter's every move could be observed—although, as it turned out, watching a young man gobble blueberry blintzes was not exactly fascinating.

"How does he do that?" asked Max.

"Eat blintzes?"

"I mean they're *hot*," said Max, *"really* hot." Between Max's cast-iron stomach and Potter's asbestos mouth, we were really quite a family.

Potter finished in no time at all and signalled the waiter for his check. I tried to signal too, but ahemming and tapping my water glass were not practical, as I wanted to attract the waiter's attention, not Potter's. I held up a finger. I raised my chin. I blinked hard. Max was more athletic; he raised his hand in the best second-grade fashion.

"Yes?"

"May we have our check, please?"

Our waiter seemed inordinately pleased with the request. He produced the check in a flash, and with equal speed, I snatched it up and then, closely followed by Max, ran down the aisle toward the cashier, where Potter was in the process of collecting his change. I slammed down a five-dollar bill.

"Let me see," said the cashier. "Hmmmm." Potter was easing through the door. "Yes, now that's three seventy-five . . . three dollars and seventy-five cents." Potter was out on the street and walking past the window. The cashier was counting on his fingers. "Three seventy-five from five makes . . . ."

"Oh, darn!" I grabbed Max's hand and bolted through the door.

Potter had not gone far. As a matter of fact, considering the amount of time he spent staring into a shoe-store window, I soon felt I had been a perfect fool to part with my dollar twenty-five in change. Eventually, however, even foot fetishists get bored. Potter walked off with his cape flapping out behind him, weaving effortlessly among the other bodies and objects on the sidewalk. Max and I followed at a respectable distance, keeping to the shadows, as Potter led us through dark, dirty streets filled with foundries and tacky corner coffee shops, before turning onto Broome Street. It was less noisy and less dirty there, and flowerpots adorned some of the windows of the big cast-iron loft buildings. Potter turned into a doorway and disappeared. A little while later, a light went on on the third floor.

Max and I leaned against a doorway across the street and waited. The focus of our attention was an ominous-looking grey building of six storeys whose exterior was distinguished by a row of columns on the ground floor and huge, dirt-covered, four-paned windows on the floors above.

"I wonder what he's doing," I sighed.

"Maybe he lives there."

From the mouth of babes. . . . I have to admit, it hadn't even occurred to me. I darted across the street with Max close behind.

"What are you *doing*?" he hissed.

"Rats!" I said. "There aren't any names listed outside

—if only we could get inside and look at the mailboxes."
Undeterred, Max reached for the doorknob and pulled,
and to my amazement, the door swung open. "What
kind of a place is this? You can't even lock the outside
door!"

"Come on," said Max. I followed him inside.

We squinted in the dim light that came through the
small window in the door and found the mailboxes.
Four of them.

"A. J. Murphy . . . N. L. . . . N. L. Edison, T. D.
Madison, and . . . W. P. Crisply." The third floor.
"Well, Max. Bingo," I said and shook his hand.

"You mean I was right? He really lives here?"

"Sure does. Come along." I figured that as long as we
had gone this far, we might as well see if we could learn
a little more, and we quietly climbed the wooden stairs,
which smelled of damp and mildew.

There was only one door on the third floor—a grey
wooden door with tarnished brass knob and peeling
paint. Luckily, there was a keyhole.

"What do you see?"

There really wasn't much to see. The keyhole exposed
only a very limited slice of the room, but it seemed to be
large and light. Mostly, I could see a section of floor that
was scratched and dirty, with old paint dried here and
there. I also saw part of a chair with one leg wired
clumsily to the seat. A dirty saucer, but no cup. An open
book. A candy wrapper.

"Here, look." Max looked for a minute and then straightened up. I could tell he was asking himself the same question I had asked myself only a minute before: Why was Potter hiding out *here*, when he could be in an uptown brownstone or a Harvard dorm? It didn't seem like the kind of place anyone would run to.

 17

Max shrugged his shoulders. I bent over to look through the keyhole once more. Of course, the view hadn't changed, but now there was the sound of walking, of clanking pans, of running water, and, perhaps, of a teakettle being placed on a stove.

"I think he's settled in for the evening," I said.

"What are we going to do?"

"There's not much we can do. . . . Wait a minute." A telephone was ringing. I put my ear to the door. Max did likewise. Again, the sound of walking, a telephone being picked up, then dropped, then picked up again. By now, I was an old hand at listening to half conversations.

"Sorry. Oh, hello! No, things are fine. . . . Everything's going according to plan . . . uh-oh . . . yes

. . . yes, it's been quite a fight; it's a jungle out there.
. . . Certainly not the place for amateurs. . . . A week
from Wednesday, if all goes well. . . . They're playing
for high stakes. . . . No, not at all . . . but it could all
be a terrible fiasco, and that's what frightens me. . . .
No, it *had* to be Wednesday night. . . . Unwarranted
interference . . . yeah, but don't let anything about
this slip; it's strictly classified information. . . ." Potter
chuckled. "Okay. Keep cool. . . . I'll see you next
Wednesday—if I'm still alive. . . . Right. Good-bye."

Potter placed the receiver back in its cradle. Max
and I looked at each other as the sound of a chair scrap-
ing across the floor came from within. "That was no ordinary phone conversation," I whispered, and we quietly
hurried down the stairs.

"Yeah," Max concurred as he closed the front door,
"and whatever he was talking about sure sounded
dangerous to me!"

 18

Max and I stood looking up at the front of our house
from across the street. Predictably, Max had also forgotten his keys. I thought about trying to break in or

picking the lock, but, since the light in my mother's second-floor study was on, both ideas were definitely out.

"Well, old chum, we're just going to have to ring the front bell, that's all. Hmmmm. Take off your hat; it won't look so suspicious."

Max immediately obeyed. However, the removal of his hat left his peculiar eye make-up exposed to view.

"On second thought, put it back on." I steeled myself for the coming confrontation. "Okay. Let's go," and hand in hand we marched across the street, up the front steps, and rang the doorbell. Max grabbed his hand away and quickly tried to cover the innumerable holes in the blue jeans he wasn't supposed to be wearing. But, considering the various other facets of our attire, that particular item was hardly the first thing our mother would be likely to notice.

We waited. Then came the sound of footsteps bounding down the stairs, the click of the peephole cover falling back into place, and the unbolting of numerous locks. The door swung open and there stood my mother.

"Yes? What can I . . . ? Well!" My mother suddenly bent down, nose to nose with Max and looked directly into his eyes as though she could peer into the darkest recesses of his soul. Max gulped and quickly removed his hat. A glimmer of a smile crossed her lips.

"Trick or treat!" she said merrily. Then she stood

up straight, folded her arms, and placed herself squarely in the doorway, blocking any possible way through. "I suppose you locked yourselves out." She stopped, obviously awaiting some further explanation, but as there appeared to be none forthcoming, she broke the silence again. "I know I shouldn't embarrass you by asking why you are dressed in that peculiar fashion . . . but I will. Why?"

"Chinese New Year," said Max. I pinched him hard.

"He's only joking. We went to a school party—a costume party." I smiled hopefully.

"Both of you?"

"Yeah. I was allowed to bring a friend."

She gave me a strange look. "Your *brother*?"

"Sure," I said. "We needed a mascot."

Max barked on cue, *very* realistically, with a bark that brought Dan hurtling down the stairs. I have never been one to let a good opportunity go to waste, so— somewhere in between Dan's charge, his lightning-like dash through the front door, and Mom's futile lunge for his collar—Max and I, with the path finally clear, ran inside and up the stairs, as fast as our little legs would go.

The aforementioned homecoming was sufficiently traumatic to keep my mother from expressing any further curiosity about our after-school activities. She seemed utterly relieved when my father showed up in a plain old business suit and tie. My father, however, noticing telltale dark circles under the eyes of a certain individual who had neglected to scrub energetically enough, found it necessary to employ all sorts of medical paraphernalia to determine whether or not the plague had hit New York. Max was finally pronounced "dirty" by the good doctor, and, after a rather quiet dinner and a good dose of homework, was sent off to dream sweet dreams. Shortly afterward, I followed suit.

 **19**

Having made our customary after-school rendezvous, Max and I walked along toward the park. I found a rather dense patch of greenery and pointed a finger. "All right, Max. Change in there. I'll keep watch," I said and motioned him toward the clump of bushes. Meanwhile, I fiddled with the clasp on my book bag—a leather monstrosity I had retired years ago but had resurrected the night before. The events of the previous evening had taught me a couple of things—first, to remember my keys, and second, to plan ahead. With this last in mind,

Max and I had carefully wadded our disguises into the bottom of our book bags (except, of course, our jackets, which we wore) before leaving for school that morning. This arrangement, which had the added benefit of giving our clothes that rumpled authenticity, had necessitated leaving a few schoolbooks behind, but this was, after all, only virtuous sacrifice in the name of a higher cause.

"Max, are you okay? Can I help?"

"No!"

A minute later, a transformed Max emerged from the shrubbery. I added the finishing touches with the makeup I had borrowed from my mother. "There. You're perfect," I said and stepped into the bushes to don my own disguise. That done, I moved our two book bags under the densest bush of the group and kicked a few of last autumn's leaves around the sides. The camouflage was excellent and it seemed fairly safe to assume that our bags would remain untouched until our return.

"Ready?"

"Ready!"

I took Max by the hand and we headed for the subway.

20

When we arrived at Potter's Broome Street residence, his lights were on and the third-floor windows were all wide open.

"Well, either he's still home or he's wasting electricity," I said, "but considering his financial status, he's almost surely home." Max and I settled down to wait in a doorway which was across the street, dark enough and far enough away to hide us from view when—and if—Potter should finally emerge.

It was a considerable amount of time before Max started to wiggle uncomfortably. "Why don't we go up and listen at the door, like before?"

"Too risky—we don't know when Potter last went out. Besides," I added, "patience is a virtue."

Patience is indeed a virtue. A minute or two later, the lights on the third floor went out. Shortly afterward, Potter opened the front door. He had on the same dark cape, the same large hat. But in one hand, he carried a large, very flat black case—a portfolio of sorts—which he rested against the wall as he paused for a moment to search in his pockets. He took out a small object and carefully flattened it against his upper lip—a fake moustache! After making sure it was securely attached, he picked up his portfolio and walked west.

Max and I were just about to step from our hiding place and follow him when something *really* amazing happened. As Potter passed a series of darkened doorways, a figure suddenly emerged from the shadows. And if Potter looked, as Max had said on the day before, something like a spy, then this gentleman looked as though he could hardly have been anything else—a middle-aged man with a long scar across one cheek and thick glasses who wore a long, dark swishing cloak and a large hat—like Potter—plus black shoes, black suit, black shirt, black tie. . . . The stranger looked around hastily and then stole quietly after Potter, darting from corner to corner and doorway to doorway to hide his presence.

"Gosh, Max! We're not the only ones following Potter . . . and our companion doesn't exactly look like the Good Fairy either." But I was not about to be frightened away. "Come on—only we've got to be very, *very* careful."

Max and I waited a moment longer and then, like an echo of the dark figure, joined in stealthy pursuit of Potter. It was unquestionably a strange parade that turned the corner of Broome Street and headed up West Broadway: two men dressed like spies, one gypsy-ish girl, and, bringing up the end of the procession, one small ragtag boy, limping because of a pebble in his shoe.

Seemingly oblivious to the motley crew he had in tow, Potter strolled along, admiring his newly mustachioed reflection in the windows of the warehouses, art galleries, and boutiques that stood side by side on West Broadway. Then suddenly, he stopped. He carefully adjusted his hat so that his eyes were disguised in shadow and after drawing his cloak tightly about him, strode up a couple of steps and into the nearest art gallery.

"Rotten time for Potter to decide he needs some culture," I mumbled.

"No, it's not," said Max and quickly extracted the pebble from his shoe.

From our hiding place down the street we watched as Potter's first follower—to whom, for lack of a better title, I shall hereafter refer as Mr. X—slithered up to the gallery building and peered in through the large windows that fronted on the street. Then he leaped to the doorway, where he continued to observe through a crack in the door. As he stood, he put his hands in his pants pockets—parting first his cape and then his jacket to reveal a revolver in a shoulder holster underneath.

"Yikes! He's not fooling around!" I thought I could feel my knees beginning to shake as bits of Potter's phone conversation ran through my head. All things considered, I was none too eager to budge—but I soon surmised that we were not going to learn a tremendous amount by watching the man who was watching Potter.

Unfortunately, Mr. X's presence in the doorway precluded any possibility of our spying through the windows that stood to either side. To the right of the gallery was another, slightly lower building containing a hardware store and radio and TV repair shop. But to the left was a parking lot.

"Okay. We're going for that lot."

Max gulped audibly.

"Listen, it'll be all right. Mr. X hasn't seen us yet, and he can't possibly have any idea that we're following him or Potter. So we'll just cross the street in an ordinary, unhurried way and he won't suspect a thing." And then I added, "I just hope it's worth the trip."

A minute later, we were in the parking lot.

"Max, we did it!"

He looked at me suspiciously. "I thought you weren't scared."

"I wasn't," I lied and breathed a sigh of relief.

"Now . . . ." I scanned the wall that faced the lot. "There!" I pointed to a window. It was relatively small and somewhat above our heads—but a row of cars had been parked with their bumpers flush to the brick, and one sat directly beneath it. I glanced around the lot quickly to make sure it was empty.

"Up you go," I said and prepared to give Max a boost.

"Beck, I can't stand on anyone's car—Mom always says . . . ." Max has altogether too many scruples.

"Under ordinary circumstances, I'd agree with you, but this is *urgent*. Now, come on." I helped Max up and climbed up beside him. Then, together, clinging with our fingertips to the rough brick of the sill, we slowly rose and peered in through the window.

Inside was a large, light room in which a number of huge, brightly coloured, abstract canvases hung against white walls. A door at the rear gave access to another, smaller room, and across the way, a flight of steps descended into the basement. A woman sat near the door typing. Otherwise, the room was empty.

A minute later, a man in a well-tailored, three-piece suit came from the back room; Potter, moustache on lip and case in hand, followed. From his proprietary manner, I judged that the man in the suit was the gallery owner.

"What are they doing? My hands hurt!" Max's fingers were purple from being pressed against the sill.

"Shhhh! I haven't the foggiest. And don't let go!"

Unfortunately, the glass of the window was too thick to enable us to hear their conversation—but then again, even an open window probably wouldn't have been much help, since they chose to do their bargaining in what appeared to be a conspiratorial whisper. Potter turned the portfolio over to the gentleman, who unzipped the case and extracted the contents. He held the sheets up one by one—from a distance they looked to be large white pages with arrows and lines, stars and boxes, inked in black and rather carefully drawn.

"Wow! What are they?"

"Hmmm. I can't say precisely—but obviously they're diagrams of some sort."

"Secret plans?"

I shrugged in answer as the gallery owner finished reviewing the pages, nodded, and tucked the whole lot under his arm. Then he and Potter shook hands and Potter, with a determined step, walked toward the front door.

"Well, here we go again." Max and I jumped down from the car and crept up to the corner of the building in time to see Mr. X, who had been lounging against the door, suddenly scurry down the steps and crouch behind them—successfully hiding everything except his hat. Potter, who emerged a second later, seemed totally unaware of the large black hat at his feet. He walked down the steps and continued on his way while our little parade re-assembled behind him. Then the four of us hurried back down West Broadway, stopping en route only long enough to enable our leader to remove his fake moustache.

It was hardly a surprise to watch Potter turn the corner onto Broome Street and disappear into his own building. Once he had gone, Mr. X tiptoed across the street and crawled into a darkened doorway. Apparently, he had decided to wait and see what would happen—and since entering Potter's building with Mr. X there was out of the question, Max and I had little choice but to do the same.

I sat down on the cold doorstep and started to mull over the facts, which, although they had once seemed relatively straightforward, had now become quite bizarre and complex. I ticked off items on my fingers as Max listened. "Okay. We know Potter has secretly been living in New York since September. We know he still loves blueberry blintzes. We know that something big is going to happen next Wednesday. And there is an important secret involved—totally aside from his living in New York." I looked at Max for confirmation.

He nodded. "Go on."

"We also know that Potter sometimes wears a disguise and that he is being followed by a suspicious character who carries a gun, looks quite mean, and is almost certainly dangerous. We know that Potter has been to an art gallery where he stopped only long enough to turn over some strange diagrams to a solemn-looking gentleman. And after leaving the premises, he removed his fake moustache—so the gallery was obviously his destination *and* the reason for his disguise, which seems to point to those documents or maps or whatever they were that Potter delivered, as the key to the whole business. All right," I said as I finished my list. "What do you make of it all?"

"Who, me? What do *you* make of it?"

"I'm glad you asked. I admit this is going to sound crazy—really crazy—but it's the only way it fits. Max, you either have extraordinary insight or you've been consulting a Ouija board, because your first guess yesterday was absolutely correct."

"It was?"

"Yes. Potter"—I paused for effect—"is a *spy.*"

Max's jaw dropped. "Oh, come on, Beck."

"Well, what else? *You* put it together."

"Maybe it's just something illegal?"

"If Potter were into something illegal, it would pay better—he wouldn't need to call home for money all the time."

Max considered this. "What about the gallery?"

"Max, my dear, things are not always what they seem. I think the gallery is only a front."

"A front?"

"What I mean is that the gallery may be a fake too: it *seems* to be an art gallery, but its real purpose is as a place to pass documents and secrets and stuff. You saw the way the gallery owner acted: he was careful and whispered to Potter, but he also took the papers openly, in full view of the lady at the desk, so she must know what's going on too. And it's my guess that it's not the first time anyone has delivered papers there either—they were all too cool about it."

"But we're not *positive* there's something funny about the papers, are we?"

"No? If there *isn't* something funny, then why did Potter go to the trouble of wearing a disguise? And if he was interested in the art, why didn't he even look at the paintings? Why did Potter and the man look like they were making a deal. Why is Mr. X following Potter? And who goes around exchanging maps and charts in a gallery anyway? Why, why, why? Is that the way *normal* people go to an art gallery?"

"No. I see your point." I think Max had to admit that although my reasoning in this whole matter led to the most fantastic conclusions, it was nonetheless based on strict logic. And you can't argue with logic.

Max was a great convert: once he had crossed the barrier of disbelief, he did not turn back. "Well, if Potter's a spy, whose side is he on?"

"Ours."

"And Mr. X?"

"Theirs."

"How do you know?"

"Well, first of all, our dear brother may be weird, brilliant, calculating, devious, deceitful"—Max nodded at each pause— "but," I said, "he is definitely *not* unpatriotic. Of that, I am absolutely sure. Besides, who looks more sinister? Potter or Mr. X?"

"Mr. X."

"There you have it. See? Potter is the good guy, and if he's the good guy, he's on our side."

Max, slightly embarrassed, asked the next question in a half whisper. "Beck, which is our side?"

"Why, Max, it's the U.S.A., of course; the CIA and all that."

"The CIA?"

"Yeah, the Central Intelligence Agency—they're our spies."

"And who are they?"

"Frankly, I suspect the Russians. I'm not certain, but that's my guess. Mr. X looks positively Slavic."

Max, seemingly overcome by the complexity and importance of all the foregoing, sighed loudly. "Well, what are we going to do?"

"Nothing yet. This puzzle still has at least a million pieces missing—but it would help if we could get to those diagrams."

"Beck . . . ."

"Shhhh!" I heard a faint rustle and put out a warning hand as I turned my attention to the doorway down the street where Mr. X was uncoiling. He crossed the street and paced back and forth in front of Potter's doorway a number of times before reaching into his holster and pulling out his gun.

"Uh-oh!"

Max crossed his fingers.

However, after tossing the gun from hand to hand a few times, Mr. X replaced it in its holster. He stood back and raised his fist in the direction of the third floor, shaking it fiercely while muttering curses to himself. And then, his anger spent, he turned on his heel, flagged a taxi that had been cruising nearby, and rode away.

"Phew!" I straightened up and stretched my legs.

Max uncrossed his fingers. "Phew!" He stepped forward, did a little dance, and then started down the street. Max tends to be a little overzealous.

"Hey! Not so fast!" I grabbed him by the collar. "We've got one. . . ." I paused.

"Huh?"

"Shhhh . . . listen," I said and pointed at the open third-floor windows as a telephone rang insistently two more times and then stopped. I nodded to Max and we both hurried across the street and up the stairs. Our ears reached Potter's door at the same time.

". . . er, yes . . . No, I told him everything would be delivered by next Monday. . . . If we're lucky, it will really stand the world on its ear. . . . Yes, yes . . . I hope nothing will go wrong. . . . Uh-huh, a real blast. . . . He's got no idea. . . . No, a disguise . . . of course. . . . There *is* no turning back. . . . On Wednesday night . . . what else? . . . top secret. . . . Okay, I'll see you then—oh, yeah . . . all the paint's dry. . . . Yes. . . . No, the colours are sensational. . . ."

So much for *that* conversation—only someone of Potter's superior intellect could, without missing a beat, skip from what sounded like a secret bombing that would change the course of world history, to interior decorating.

"No, I'd like to kill him. . . ." My ears perked up again. "But of course . . . it's *the* big chance. . . . The United States. . . . Nothing had better go wrong, or else. . . . Ha, ha . . . yeah, wish me luck. . . . Yes, you too. . . . See you Wednesday night. Right. Bye." As I said, he doesn't miss a beat.

Potter hung up and all was quiet within. Max and I descended quickly and were soon out in the street and on our way to the subway.

"Well, Max. I'd say that conversation confirmed everything. Especially . . . ."

Max tugged at my sleeve. "Don't you think we should tell someone?"

I stopped for a moment and thought seriously. "No,

Max. I think it would be a grave mistake. Suppose we got the police involved in this; suppose they were to bust in on the middle of a top-secret government mission and ruin everything. I doubt anyone would thank us for that. I think we've got to assume that Potter knows what he's doing—but I also think we ought to hang around, just in case."

 **22**

After a quick change of clothes in the bushes and the judicious application of water from the park fountain and a little soap, we headed for home. I closed the front door quietly, but my mother has ears like a bat. My father was home too.

"My, my. You're out awfully late," my mother's voice floated out from the kitchen.

"Yes, too bad you missed dinner," said my father, who came out and leaned against the wall. Max looked horrified. "Sorry. Only kidding. What would you like your ketchup on tonight?"

"Chicken?"

"Will you settle for pork chops?"

"Mmmmmm." Max rubbed his stomach and patted his head—a trick he had mastered at age two and a half.

"Well, it's almost ready, so wash up quickly."

"We already have. . . ." I threw Max a dirty look and dragged him out of the room. We let the water in the basin run noisily for a minute or two before returning downstairs and sliding into our usual seats.

"What did you do today?" My father, who is fond of meaningful dinner table conversations, looked at Max.

"Went to school," said Max, mouth full.

My mother rested her head on her clasped hands. "Fascinating. Absolutely fascinating."

"And?"

"And that's *all*." (I was preparing to silence Max with a kick under the table.)

"I mean, what did you do *in* school?"

Max looked around quickly. "Did Miss Altowitz call?"

"Well. . . ." My father paused, waiting.

Max swallowed. "I didn't really want to do it."

For a moment, I contemplated saving Max from himself—but this was getting interesting.

"I know you didn't mean it," said my mother slyly, "but your father doesn't—so why don't you explain it to him?"

My father was drumming his fingers on the table and trying not to break out laughing, but I think this last subtlety escaped Max. He gulped. "I . . . um . . . I ate twelve pink erasers." Leave it to Max.

"You what?" My mother looked as if she were going to be ill.

"It was a dare. I've got twenty-five cents."

"You've got no financial sense—well, like father, like son." My father rose suddenly and left the table, returning a minute later with his black doctor's bag. "Do we open him up now or later?" He looked at my mother.

"On the kitchen table? Not a chance!" She folded her arms stubbornly.

My father took a long steel instrument out of his bag. "I've never performed an eraserectomy before." He smiled maniacally and fingered the blade. Max, who was beginning to think that perhaps they were not joking, started to edge away from the table. But then, of course, they burst out laughing and gave it away. My father put down his bag. "Listen, Max, it's okay, but next time, for the honour of the family, would you show a little restraint? Wouldn't three have been enough?"

Max let out a long sigh and laughed too. "Right, Dad," he said and unclutched his stomach.

 **23**

I was sitting at the kitchen table the next morning, trying to polish off the rest of my maths homework, when Max arrived downstairs. My mother turned from the stove with a spatula in one hand and a salt shaker in the other. "Max, comb your hair, dear. It looks awful."

For what must have been the second time that morning, Max ran his fingers through his hair, and then sat down.

"You're up early," I said. Max still had forty-five minutes left to sleep before he had to get up for school, which was precious time indeed. Besides, Max looked half dead.

"I know," he said, "Dan," and slumped across the table.

I nodded sympathetically. Dan always woke up at the sound of my father's alarm and, having stoically spent the night on the floor in the hall, usually assumed that it was his right to claim a reward of a few minutes on someone's bed. This was fine if he happened to pick my father's bed, which was by then unoccupied, but all too often, Dan perversely chose a bed that had not been vacated. And Dan is no lap dog.

I removed Max's limp hand from my homework and filled in the last answer.

"Well," my mother said cheerily, "have a good night's sleep?" Max didn't move. "Here, drink this. It will make you feel better," she said and put a glass of orange juice into his hand.

Max took the glass, sat up slowly, and swallowed its

contents. As he did so, the colour gradually returned to his face—it would have made a great commercial for o.j.—and he looked quite normal by the time my mother placed plates of fried eggs, toast, and bacon before each of us. Having thus provided her offspring with an incontrovertibly well-balanced and nutritious breakfast, she hung up her apron. "I'm going upstairs to change. Oh, and Becky, I'll be home late tonight—it's the spring faculty meeting. I think your father will be home at a reasonable hour, but just in case, don't forget to feed Dan and Armenia, please." She smiled and dashed out the door.

Max was engaged in carefully rearranging his breakfast plate: two fried eggs for eyes, a slice of bacon for a nose, and a toast mouth—one triangle with the middle point down, smiling, of course. Positively charming. However, Max took care of this latest masterpiece by gobbling it down immediately upon completion. That done, he hooked his legs around the legs of the kitchen table and tilted back precariously in his chair.

"Beck, if Potter is a spy, does that mean he isn't going to be a doctor any more?"

"Hmmmm." I wasn't sure whether spying could properly be considered a career or not. I tried to imagine Potter, old and grey, still wearing his long cloak and a fake moustache. But, bizarre as the image was, I had to admit there was a distinct possibility that Potter might never present Mom and Dad with a medical school diploma to hang above his bronzed baby shoes.

"I don't know, Max," I answered. "Maybe he'll finish school later."

"Well," Max said and tilted back in his chair a little farther, "it's still pretty neat. Richard McNulty's brother is a college quarterback—but that's not nearly as cool as having a brother who works for the CIA."

"That's right, Max. But just be sure you don't go blabbing that particular bit of information all over. It wouldn't do for the whole second grade to know."

"Sure, Beck," Max called as I left the room. "I'll see you this afternoon, same time, same—" but his sentence was interrupted by the thud of a chair falling to the floor.

 24

One of the nice things about our disguises was that the more we wore them, the more dirty and realistic they—and we—looked. It was evident that no one on the subway car would ever have guessed that Max might be a middle-class kid from a good home. A huge woman in curlers shuddered as Max sat down next to her and quickly inched her way down the bench, as a man in painter's overalls, to Max's left, muttered something about "revolting infestation" and leaped for a free seat across the aisle. I promised myself that in the future, I'd go a little easier on Max's eye shadow.

After leaving the subway, we walked over to Broome Street and then cautiously moved along the sidewalk until we found a comfortable corner in which to hide. The lights in Potter's windows were on. In the course of many minutes, I changed positions once, twice, three times.

"Did you hear that?"

"What?"

And then someone yawned again, quite audibly this time. And whoever it was was in the doorway right beside us! Mr. X, who had apparently just finished a snooze, got up and yawned once more. He stepped into the light to check his watch, and then, crouching, moved off down the street with as much stealth and care as his very squeaky shoes would allow. He resettled himself in another doorway, directly across the street from Potter's.

Max, who had been holding his breath, took a deep one. "That was close."

"Yes, almost *too* close." I shivered as I tried to imagine exactly what Mr. X might have done with us, but my mind was mercifully diverted from this train of thought by the sudden extinguishing of the lights on the third floor. Potter, of course, emerged shortly thereafter—with the usual black cape and big hat, and the large black case. His moustache had already been applied. With an air of great self-assurance, Potter started to walk down Broome Street—followed quickly by his tenacious little band of admirers.

"Potter sure is something," whispered Max.

I watched Potter as he strode on, betraying not the slightest trace of fear. "That, Max, has to be the most nonchalant spy in the world."

"Yeah," said Max. "Wow."

I had expected Potter to return to the gallery, but our imperturbable spy was taking us on a route leading east rather than west, so he obviously had other plans. Accordingly, some minutes later we crossed Canal Street and started down Mulberry. And there we were, in Chinatown. Another world.

Potter led us along narrow streets flanked by five- and six-storey tenement buildings and lined with the makeshift stands of dozens of fruit and vegetable sellers. His tall, cloaked figure looked out of place as he sauntered down the crowded sidewalks, stopping here and there to gaze into the windows of the many small food shops—windows filled with tins of exotic teas and spices, crisp cooked chickens, lovely pink and yellow tea cakes . . . . by the time we got to Mott Street, I was beginning to feel very nostalgic about our after-school snack. Apparently, Max was beginning to feel the same way. He pulled at my sleeve.

"Couldn't we stop and get just one little cooky?"

It was tempting—but I was not about to lose Potter over "one little cooky."

I turned around. "Not now, Max. We've got more important things to do."

When I turned back to look up the street, to my horror, Potter was gone. "Max, did you see where he went?"

"Uh-uh." Max was still gazing into a bakery window.

"Come on. He can't have gone very far," I said. Fortunately, we didn't have to look very far. The black-caped Mr. X, who had until now kept a relatively low profile, turned out to be as good as a road sign. He was standing in front of a bookstore a little way down, where he deliberated for a moment before choosing a foothold on the wall of the low building, scrabbling up the side, and disappearing over the top—having evidently decided to expend his energy on a rear assault.

Max looked at me. "You know," he said, "Mr. X is a rotten spy."

I had begun to suspect the same thing, but I thought I'd be charitable. "Maybe he expects Potter to escape through a back door." Whatever the reason for the acrobatics, his exit left the front of the building clear, enabling us to watch Potter more easily. We hurried across the street and knelt down among the wooden crates and strange vegetables of a sidewalk stand. The stand's owner looked at us impatiently and said something in rapid Chinese. But as he made no attempt to bodily evict us, we stayed put. It was the perfect stake-out: Max looked like a big piece of celery.

The Chinatown Book Company was a long, narrow store. We could see Potter clearly through the window, talking to a man at the counter and then, it seemed, paying for some item. They smiled and shook hands and continued in conversation for a while before Potter finally emerged with his purchase—a long, thin bamboo brush.

"He came all the way down here for *that*?" Max asked in an irritated voice.

I shrugged. Potter examined the brush carefully and started to walk down Mott Street. Mr. X was nowhere to be seen.

"Something's different about Potter." I looked closely, but I couldn't pinpoint anything: he was still wearing his cape and hat, he still had his fake moustache. He entered a bakery a few doors down and reappeared a minute later carrying a huge cooky in the form of a fat, smiling man. In a sadistic move, he bit off the head. Max watched hungrily.

Suddenly, Potter stopped in mid-bite and stowed the

unfinished cooky in his pocket. He retraced his steps to the bookstore.

"Of course! The case!" I don't know how I'd missed it before, but now, as the gentleman stepped from the doorway of the bookstore to hand Potter his portfolio, I was amazed that I had failed to notice its absence. Potter accepted the case, thanked the man, and went back along Mott Street, slowly munching his decapitated cooky. And wherever Mr. X had gone, he seemed—for lack of evidence to the contrary—to still be there.

"Hey," said Max. "Did he mean to do that?"

"Leave his case behind? . . . He could have just forgotten it. Then again . . . then again, it could be a clever way of exchanging secret documents."

"That's what *I* thought," said Max.

"Hmmm. Very sly," I mused. "He goes in to buy a token item and 'forgets' the portfolio. Then his contact goes to the back room, extracts the contents—or fills it with papers for Potter to deliver elsewhere—and it all looks totally innocent."

"So the Chinese are involved too?"

"Huh?"

"It's just that you said it was us and the Russians, but are the Chinese involved in—in whatever it is?"

"Hmmmm. That's an interesting idea. I don't know if I'd rule it in exactly, but I definitely wouldn't rule it out."

As usual, we had a lot of questions—but the most immediate one was: Where was Potter taking us now? The answer turned out to be the Chinatown Fair and Museum, a large building situated near the end of Mott Street. One look inside and I got the awful feeling that Potter might waste the rest of the afternoon playing pinball—which was not such an absurd notion, considering the fact that this particular establishment was filled with pinball machines, video games, automated shooting galleries, and other equally seductive equipment. However, such fears were premature because, as we soon discovered, Potter was *really* after Clara, the Fortune-Telling Chicken!

Max and I watched from the shadows of an automated hockey machine as Potter took a coin from his pocket and dropped it in a slot. A bell sounded and Clara, a real live chicken, did a little dance and then pulled a cord with her beak which caused a printed card to shoot from an opening in her box. For her effort, Clara got chickenfeed; for his money, Potter got the fortune. He read the card quickly and laughed before tossing it way and walking out the door.

Every-ready Max dived for the discarded fortune and in the process almost knocked over a surprised hockey player, between whose knees he had lunged. He apologized quickly and stood up.

"Here, I can't read it. The words are too big." He held

the slip out to me as I poked my nose out the door to see where Potter had gone. But he had only moved a few yards away and was standing with one shoe off, trying to straighten out his sock.

I took the card from Max. " 'He whose artifice is artless is the most artful of all.' "

"What's it supposed to mean?"

"Nothing," I snapped. "It's not some secret message; it's just a silly old fortune card. And it's not supposed to mean anything—they *pay* people to think up enigmas."

"To think up whats?"

"Never mind."

"But Potter thought the card was funny."

"Well, *he's* weird! Come on."

Max hung back. "Can't we put a nickel in?"

"Max!" I groaned.

"Please? Please, Beck?" Among his other notable characteristics, I should have mentioned that my little brother is embarrassingly superstitious. I looked around the corner again. Potter was now repeating the same operation with his other shoe and sock.

"Okay. Here—quickly." I handed Max a nickel. He dropped it into the coin slot and handed me the card.

" 'Beware of those who fear the sun and live in shadow.' Well, at least that one's easy," I said. "Beware of Mr. X. It seems to me, however, that Clara is worrying herself needlessly, in view of the recent level of competence he's displayed. Thank you anyway, Clara. And come on, Max. Fortune-telling time is over."

I pocketed the cards and we headed for the street, where Potter, who had finally solved his podiatric problems, was ambling along. The black-caped form of the once redoubtable—and recently returned—Mr. X could be seen close behind.

Our stalwart group travelled back up Mott Street and across busy Canal Street, where we almost lost Max under a careering pedal wagon driven by a crazed delivery boy. But with a little luck—and a big push—Max made it safely across the street and into Little Italy. Good-bye Chinatown. The smell of pizza was devastating.

"Doesn't he do anything except eat?" Max groaned as Potter turned the corner and entered Ferrara's, a well-stocked Italian bakery. We could see him pointing out his choice of pastries to a man behind the counter.

"Sure," I sneered. "He talks to fortune-telling chickens. For a man who's got a date with destiny next Wednesday, he sure is taking his time about things."

Max rubbed the heel of his right foot. "Yeah, and thanks to him, I've got more blisters now than toes."

"Well," I said and happily wiggled my own, "that will teach you to laugh at white tennis sneakers."

Max scowled. "What's he doing in there? Do you think he's exchanging more papers?"

"Could be—but in this case, I'm quite positive that things are exactly as they appear to be."

"As they appear to be?"

"It's alimentary, my dear Max. Alimentary."

"Huh?"

"Forget it, Max."

"I think I will."

 **25**

After leaving Ferrara's, Potter headed uptown to the gallery and we watched him now as he stood outside the building, checking his moustache to make sure that it was still properly affixed. Finding everything in order, he marched up the steps. Exit Potter. Of course, Mr. X immediately took up his watch by the front door, while Max and I, on the correct side of the street for a change, slipped into the parking lot, unseen.

Unfortunately, we soon discovered that we had a small problem—there was a large space underneath our window where there should have been a car. Obviously, one of us had to stand on the other's shoulders and I wasn't any too eager to trust this mission to Max's untrained eye. On the other hand, I knew it wouldn't really be sporting to ask Max to let me stand on his shoulders, since I am almost twice his size. So, I stood, uncomplaining, as Max climbed up my back, and knelt on my shoulders.

"Pssst! What do you see?" Max has very sharp knees.

"Well . . . ," Max whispered, as he looked down and leaned away from the wall.

"Don't look at me! Just talk!"

"Ummm. Potter's shaking hands with the same man. They're talking . . . and he's giving him the portfolio. . . . No, he's still holding it. Potter's showing him what's inside—it . . . it looks like the diagrams we saw yesterday. Oh, and . . . ." Max moved too quickly and jabbed a knee into my head. I immediately stumbled backward. Luckily, Max landed to one side, rather than *on* my head, when I fell.

"Max!" I hissed.

"Sorry." He looked positively contrite.

I rubbed my ear and looked up at the window. However, as I was in the middle of contemplating whether to take on arrow-kneed Max again or to tempt fate and try inverted proportions, my eyes fell upon a door at the other end of the wall. Of course, a door wasn't of much use to us, since we couldn't risk opening it, but this particular door just happened to be beside a ladder— and a ladder is a very useful thing indeed. It was anchored to the side of the one-storey building and went straight up to the roof.

"Well, that's more like it," I said. "How very thoughtful of them." And to Max's amazement—he was sure I was going to punch him—I took him gently by the hand and led him up the ladder.

The roof was flat and sturdy, and we crept across it very carefully, making hardly any sound. We headed for the middle, where there was a large wooden frame, a sort of hatch door that opened upward, and someone had obligingly propped it open a few inches to allow fresh air to circulate.

"We're in luck," I whispered softly. We could hear the voices below quite clearly, but we could not see much of anything through the crack—at least from that angle. I leaned over a bit. Max did the same thing—and somehow managed to slip against the hatch.

He jumped back. "I . . . ."

"Shhhh!"

The door swayed slightly, but there was no sign from within that anyone had noticed Max's potentially disastrous mistake.

"Be *careful!*" I mouthed.

"I *was* being careful. I just slipped, that's all."

I glared at Max a moment longer and then turned my attention back to the conversation downstairs.

". . . Yes, well, I do like what you've brought me," I heard someone say. I tapped Max on the shoulder.

"Who was in the room?"

"Potter, the lady, and the same man."

"That's all?"

"Yup."

Since it was a male voice and not Potter's, I deduced that it must be the gallery owner speaking.

OWNER: "It is, however, not exactly what you promised me."

POTTER: "It's all I have now. It's actually better than the other stuff. I can make another delivery next week . . . [inaudible] . . . could be arranged . . ."

OWNER: "Forget it. There's plenty here . . . all we need to do a bang-up job . . . quite a good deal . . . I hope you get your reward. . . . yes . . . yes, if those cutthroats leave you alone. . . . Wednesday night."

POTTER: "I'm not scared of them. . . . sure, I'll be here early. . . . Oh, don't do that. . . . Wednesday night."

OWNER: "What about your government . . . ?"

POTTER: ". . . government . . . old Uncle Sam. . . . Yes, I think so too. . . . It's a sure thing."

The rest of the talk was conducted in such soft voices that we lost most of it and, in fact, only realized that it had ended when we heard the clear sounds of one person—undoubtedly Potter—walking toward the front door.

86

"Let Potter and Mr. X go," I said as Max started for the ladder.

"Huh?"

"I think Potter's going home. And I say we'd do better to stick around here and explore a little more, especially since I was right about the gallery. . . ." I stopped as I heard the sound of the door closing and waited until I was sure that Potter and Mr. X had gone. Then Max and I climbed down into the parking lot.

"Anyway, as I was saying, I'm positive I was right about the gallery being a front. It's probably a big centre of operations."

"A centre for who? The CIA?"

"No, Max. Think. If Potter works for the CIA and wears a disguise to the gallery, then the gallery—and the gallery owner—can't be connected with the CIA. Right?"

"Right—I guess." Max looked at me expectantly.

"Okay. . . . But since the gallery owner seems to *think* that Potter is on his side, then that means that—get this—Potter must be a *double* agent."

"Potter's two spies in one?"

"Sort of. And if he's trying to mislead them about his identity, he's also undoubtedly passing phony documents to the gallery owner, Mr. G—G for 'gallery.' "

"*G* for 'good,' " said Max.

"What?"

"*G* for 'good, I'm glad he's not on our side.' He looks

nasty—like Mr. X." Max thought that one over for a second. "Hey, Beck? Are *they* on the same side?"

"I guess not—if they were, Mr. X wouldn't have to stand outside the gallery and spy. Hmmm. . . . That means we've got three groups involved in this—at the very least."

"And you still think Mr. X is Russian?"

"I'm not sure," I said. "He looks Russian, but we don't know if he sounds Russian because we haven't heard him speak. We do know that he's not a very good spy."

"And his shoes squeak. . . ."

". . . which is another good point, because the Russians are notorious for poorly made consumer goods, baggy suits and squeaky shoes included. Did you notice his suit?"

"It's pretty hard to see much underneath his cape, but it was a sort of normal suit, I think—if you like black —maybe a little baggy."

"Well, we'll look more closely next time. Now, whatever else you can say about our other friend, Mr. G, *his* clothes aren't baggy. He was rather impeccably dressed."

"And he doesn't have a foreign accent."

"So either he has lost all trace of his foreign origins . . . or he's a traitor."

"Yeah . . . a *traitor*," Max repeated uneasily—it's the sort of word that can send shivers up and down anyone's spine.

26

Max and I were crouched in a corner across the street, looking at the gallery for telltale signs. There were two big plate-glass windows out front on either side of a windowless double door. There were also two small windows at sidewalk level that let light into the basement.

"Look carefully, Max. What do you see?"

Max frowned and pushed his hat back slightly on his head. "Well, there's a wire over there that goes from the gallery to the hardware store. There are two trash cans that are almost full. And there's a smokestack or something that's pretty tall, and it comes out of the back of the roof." Max looked at me for approval.

"All right," I said, "and there is also a red and yellow banner outside the gallery, above the door. And then there's the gallery name—did you notice?" I think Max, who was after all only a fledgling reader, had skipped that detail on purpose. "The Two Continents Gallery." I read the sign solemnly and then started to cross the street.

"Beck! They'll see you!"

"It's okay, Max. They couldn't possibly know who we are. It's perfectly safe."

"That's what you said the last time."

"Well, *this* time, I mean it," I said and started to walk again. Max, who quickly decided that crossing the street with me, whatever the perils, was infinitely better than standing on the opposite kerb by himself, fell into step.

Once on the other side, I scanned the front wall for more clues. There was a buzzer to one side of the door and some old posters taped to the brick, although only about half remained of any of them. I smoothed down the edges of the first:

Greek Va
of the
August 5–Au
    and
Western waterc
Indians

Then another:

Two Conti
West Broad
Texas Ti
Robert S
    and
French pas
XIXth

There was a third:

Two Con
West Br
November 6–
Jan Erd
Californ
recent graph
    and
Art of Ru
Icons and mos

There was a picture on the last one—part of a mosaic.

Max, who has enough trouble reading whole words, looked utterly baffled by these fragments. I translated the last one:

"Two Continents—that's this gallery." I turned to Max. "See? All you have to do is fill in the blanks. There's the address—West Broadway—and the date, which must have been last fall, and this part says, 'a show of recent graphic work by a California artist named Jan something.' Got it?" Max didn't say anything, so I continued, "Jan something, *plus* icons and mosaics—you can see from the picture—or the art of Ru, which . . . ."

"What's the art of Ru?" Max interrupted.

"I was about to . . . . Never mind. Guess."

"Um . . . Rembrandt?"

I could tell that Rembrandt was the only artist Max knew. "Not 'Re,' 'Ru,'" I said, "and 'Ru' is not just Ru; it's the first part of *Russia*."

"Wow," said Max. "How do you know?"

"Who else has icons and begins with 'Ru'?" Max did not mention anything about not knowing what an icon was, so I let it go at that.

"Gee, Russia," Max repeated, "I wish *I* could read like that."

"I wish you could too—it would save me a lot of trouble." I gazed at the posters a minute longer. "I suppose that's where the 'Two Continents' comes in—it's a gallery that shows both foreign and American art at the same time . . . interesting." I released the edges of the paper, and the poster immediately re-curled.

"Okay, next step." After quickly checking through the gallery windows to make sure that no one was watching us—the lady was typing, and Mr. G was nowhere to be seen—I bent down. Max joined me on hands and knees as I rubbed a little of the dirt off the glass of the basement window. It was an ordinary sort of basement: dimly lit and dusty. There were a lot of boxes stacked about, as well as some large canvases covered with sheeting which were propped up against a wall. To one side, a stairway led up to gallery level. And at the rear, there was a door. It was padlocked and a sign—which I could read at that distance only because it had been

printed in such large letters—said: ABSOLUTELY NO AD-
MITTANCE.

"Certainly sounds hospitable." I stood up and moved
toward the door.

"Where are we going?"

"Into the gallery."

If Max had looked somewhat hesitant before about
crossing the street, he now looked positively horrified.
"Uh-uh. Not me."

"Yes, you," I said. "Believe me, Max. It's okay."

"How about if I stand outside and wait?"

"Nothing doing. Are we partners or not?"

"Uh . . . partners."

"Then come on, and stop acting like a baby." I pulled
the handle on one side of the heavy door, and it swung
open. And Max, who had straightened up to his full
height, stepped into the gallery with me.

The lady at the front desk looked up. She eyed us
both from top to toe. "Yes?"

"We'd just like to look around—uh, at the paintings—
if it's okay."

"Yes," said the lady. "It's okay," but she continued
to stare. I guess we didn't look like your typical, run-
of-the-mill, afternoon gallery-goers. I took Max over to
one of the large canvases and pretended to look at it
closely. I tilted my head to the side as if I were very
interested, although the painting was not very interest-

93

ing at all—just a lot of colour splashed all over. Personally, I preferred Max's finger paintings.

"That's an Alfred Ornstickler," the lady's voice said behind us.

"I know," I lied and untilted my head on the theory that perhaps I had looked a little too interested.

I was in the middle of examining the picture frames for suspicious details when the phone on the desk rang. The lady jumped for the receiver. "Hello? Oh. . . ." And she quickly switched into a foreign language full of weird inflections and strange pronunciations. I looked at Max.

"Russian?" he whispered.

"Well," I said. "It sure ain't French." Actually, "gibberish" would have been a perfect classification. Max held on to my hand tightly as we manoeuvred our way around to the rear of the gallery and stopped by the door to the back room. It had been left open and a number of large sheets were lying on the desk.

Max tugged at my sleeve. "Beck," he whispered.

"Huh?"

"That's them. That's what Potter had in his hand today."

"Good work, Max," I said and inched a bit closer. The top page was covered with a number of arrows and dotted lines, like the ones on the sheets we'd seen previously. And although I could not make out all the details, I could also see some funny little circles drawn here and there and a colour photograph of, of all things, the Empire State Building, glued down in one corner.

What we needed now was to get a really good look at the diagrams. I glanced at the front desk and started to inch around the corner into the back room. And then— I would have sworn that the room was empty—Mr. G suddenly swung around the corner of the filing cabinet. I almost fell into his arms.

"Pardon me," he said gruffly, "but this room is private. There's *no* admittance."

"Oh," I said, "ah . . . I was just looking for the . . . um, drinking fountain."

"Haven't got one," Mr. G said and marched past me. He just about fell over Max too.

"I suppose you were also looking for the drinking fountain," he sneered.

"Y-y-yes, sir."

"Well, we *still* haven't got one," he said and closed the door to the back room with a slam. Then he walked hastily to the front, pulled open the door, and was gone. I thought it might be about time for Max and me to make our exit too—especially as the gallery seemed to have yielded up all its readily accessible clues, few though they were.

We moseyed toward the door. "Nice Alfred Ornsticklers," I said just loudly enough. "Real nice."

The lady at the desk smiled. "Would you like a glass of water?" Eavesdropper. She reached for a pitcher on the shelf behind her and poured out a glass.

"Um . . . thank you." It was lukewarm, and I forced myself to take a couple of sips. However, the drink did give me time to glance around the desk, where I noticed a stack of postcards with a reproduction of a painting printed on each one. Gallery announcements.

Recent Work by Alfred Ornstickler; Two Continents Gallery; March 10–April 20. Gallery Director—James Nassur.

"May I have one?"

"Certainly," the lady answered and started pounding away at her typewriter once more. I took two, mumbled another thank-you, and hurried out the door.

It was terribly quiet on the street—the only living soul seemed to be the man with the pretzel wagon who was standing directly in front of the gallery. Max, remembering the after-school snack he hadn't had, tried to look his most pathetic.

"Beck?"

"Okay. Go ahead." I handed him some change which was soon exchanged for a slightly misshapen pretzel. Then we started off for the subway.

"You know, I've been thinking."

"What?" Max said through an overly large bite.

"That was a pretty strange pretzel man. He's all the

way down here with almost no one to sell pretzels to. And another thing, that cart—it was *too* clean. Pretzel carts are never antiseptic." I noticed that Max wasn't chewing with such gusto any more. "Besides, that guy only charged fifteen cents, and everywhere else in the city, pretzels cost a quarter. But the clincher is that he wasn't selling chestnuts. When was the last time you saw a pretzel man who didn't sell chestnuts?"

Max swallowed his mouthful with some difficulty. "Never."

"You want to know what I think?"

Max shook his head.

"Well, I think that he works for *them*. He's not a *real* pretzel man—he's their *lookout*."

Max looked green. "Do you think he poisoned the pretzel?"

"Only if that lady poisoned the water."

Max seemed immensely comforted by the thought that if one of us were to drop dead, the other would too.

"But if he's a lookout, why didn't he look out for us?"

"Because they're not trying to keep *everyone* out of the gallery, just the wrong people—and they haven't figured out yet that we're the wrong people."

27

Max was lagging behind, as usual. I stopped to let him catch up. "Your leg is sticking out."

"Huh?"

"The leg of your blue jeans—it's caught."

Max looked down at the offending bit of material, stopped, and stuffed it back into his book bag.

"Come here a second. You also left a smudge under your eye." I held Max firmly with one hand and rubbed at it gently, but it would not come off. "Oh, well, it makes you look like an authentic seven-year-old." We continued walking.

"We're really going to catch it tonight, Max."

"It's really late, isn't it?"

I looked at my watch for the umpteenth time. It's not that my parents really care where we are or even what we do; it's just that at a certain point, like any self-respecting parents, they feel obligated to call the police and report a kidnapping.

"Know any compelling lies?" I asked.

Max just scuffed along.

Actually, I needn't have worried so, for at that moment, there were things happening at home that would make our late arrival seem trivial by comparison.

We had already turned onto our block and were only a short distance away from the house, when I noticed something peculiar. My mother—or someone with her silhouette—was standing on the stoop talking to a man. The second figure was fairly tall and had a long cape— my eyes were just beginning to adjust to the dim light— and . . . . "Max! It's Mr. X!" There was no mistaking that sinister profile. Max's jaw dropped a good two inches. He watched, bug-eyed, as Mr. X, who had finished his nefarious business, swished his cloak in an ominous way, turned abruptly, and scurried off into the night.

"What was *he* doing here?" Max's eyes were still half out of his head.

"Max, don't you know? Can't you see? He must be threatening Mom and Dad to get information about Potter. He thinks they know something!"

"Gee," said Max.

"Come on. We'd better get inside." I took hold of Max's hand; it was as cold as ice.

28

I closed the door softly, even though I knew my mother would hear us come in. However, she was deeply immersed in a conversation with my father and made no comment—although they did stop talking a moment after we entered.

I put my book bag down and took off my parka. "Who was that?" I asked as offhandedly as I could.

"Who was who?" said my father.

"The man who just left."

"Oh, *him*," said my mother and glanced quickly at my father. "Cable TV. He wanted to know if we wanted cable TV."

"Can we?" asked Max with enthusiasm. Sometimes his ability to concentrate on the issues at hand amazes me.

"It appears to me," said my father, relaxing a little, "that all our minds have been sufficiently corrupted. After all, we wouldn't want to overdo a bad thing." Max, who had been getting lousy reception on his favourite programme, "Marvin the Mighty Man," for two weeks now, looked crestfallen.

"Well, children," my mother said with what seemed to me to be forced cheeriness, "I'm going to make us all a lovely dinner."

"I'll help," said my father, and they excused themselves and slipped off to the kitchen, debating something in hushed tones as they went.

My mother has tremendous equilibrium. In spite of Mr. X's unexpected and troubling visit, she somehow managed to get dinner on the table. It was even good. Of course, nothing further was said that evening about the man from cable TV.

"How's school going, Max?" my mother asked. I thought that we had already been through this one the night before, but there is no rest for the weary. Poor Max. The tips of his ears turned red, but he just sawed away at his steak without looking up.

"Excuse me," said my father, "but you're using your knife upside down—you get an A-plus for effort, though."

Max turned his knife over and continued to ignore my mother's question.

"You know," my mother cooed softly, "you are our brightest child. . . ." She was obviously feeling for a soft spot. Max smiled hesitantly, but he was beginning to shift uneasily in his chair. "I know," she continued, "because all our other children—you remember your sister, Rebecca, and your brother, Potter?—used to take their schoolbooks to school with them. But I presume you've already memorized yours. Or tell me, is there another reason why you left them at the bottom of the clothes hamper?"

Only Max would have thought of that.

"Um, I didn't need those books today."

"Well, neither did Rachel. She says they ran when she put them in the wash—and they're *murder* to iron."

"Sorry," said Max.

"Tomorrow," my father announced, "I'm going to invent the bookcase—well, that is, after I finish the wheel—and the day after, I think I'll work on fire, and then maybe . . . ."

"How about a dishwasher?" suggested my mother. She's been needling him about one for years.

"Oh," said my father, "that's easy. I've been working on *that* for thirteen years," and he flashed a charming smile in my direction.

"Not bad," said my mother. "Now let's see if it works."

 **29**

I handed Max another plate and he mopped at it with the one partly dry square inch left on his dish towel. He had become so proficient that my father had permanently promoted him to Number One Dish Dryer. I was still working on a plan to get him into the Number One Washer's spot.

"Tell me, Max—why did you decide to hide your books in the clothes hamper?"

"Mom would have noticed if I'd put them in my bookcase—my arithmetic book is bright red."

"So you put them in the hamper. Of course, where else?"

"How was I supposed to know that Rachel was going to rat on me?"

I thought that I had better see to it that Rachel did not get the opportunity to rat again, so, after finishing the dishes, I explained to Max the virtues of a certain dusty shelf in the hall closet. Obviously, no one had touched it in months. It was so untouched, in fact, that I found my English notebook from the year before under a stack of hand towels. Now, the only interesting thing about this notebook was that it was almost blank. It had been a very slow year in English—six months on *Huckleberry Finn* (they don't want to get too pushy in my school) and the rest on a poem by Alfred, Lord Tennyson. And it just so happened that the thing I needed most at that very moment was a blank—or almost blank—notebook.

I took it into my room and in one deft motion tore out the extraneous material on Mark Twain and A. L. T. Max watched, speechless—obviously horrified by this sacrilege.

"Now," I said, "I am going to write down *everything*.

This whole affair has gotten so convoluted that I can't keep anything straight any more." I looked at Max. "Are you confused?" He sort of bobbed his head around in a circle, confirming my suspicions that he was so confused, he didn't know if he was confused.

"All right, then. Let's get to work. First . . . ." And I began to write.

A few minutes later, after listing all our clues under four major categories headed POTTER, MR. X, MR. G, and GALLERY, I settled back to gaze at my handiwork. I had hoped that with everything written down, things would miraculously fall into logical—and intelligible—order. No such luck.

"Okay, Max. . . ." I stopped. There was a scratching sound at my door, and then I heard a long, low, sorrowful whine. I flipped my notebook shut, and Max got up and opened the door. It was—I should have known—the great and heroic dog of the manse, making his nightly rounds with the *New York Times* in his mouth. Dan dropped it at my feet and sat down, panting. Once, long ago, in a fit of boredom, my mother had taught Dan how to carry the paper in his mouth. *She* had assumed that our faithful hound would simply transport it from the front hall to the living room. *Dan* had assumed that she wanted him to tote the *Times* around forevermore and guard it properly. That had upset my father terribly—and since Dan and my father have never learned to share, we now get two copies of the *New York Times* delivered every day.

"Dan, go away," I said. He looked like he was eyeing my precious tennis sneakers. Max, with great presence of mind, quickly shoved the *Times* back into Dan's mouth and threw man's best friend out the door. Then he resumed his place and peered over my shoulder.

"Thank you," I said and opened my notebook once more.

I sat drumming my pencil over the column labelled MR. X.

"Hey, Beck, will you go over that again?" Max asked.

"Sure. It's quite simple. All I was really saying is that Mr. X is *not* our Russian."

"But you said . . . ."

"I've revised my opinion."

"He had squeaky shoes," I was reminded.

"Max, there are lots of squeaky shoes in this world. But, here's the way I figure it: The Russians are big and powerful, they have lots of money and incredible resources at their command, and they can definitely afford to hire a competent spy—which, as we've come to agree, Mr. X is not. What the Russians *would* do is to establish an operation like the gallery with a good, inconspicuous staff, a pretzel man for a lookout, and the perfect arrangement for passing goods and documents."

"What arrangement?"

105

"Two Continents," I said. "Get it? Art work from overseas? Look, when they need to transport secret papers and stuff, they stash whatever it is in the picture frames, or the base of statues, or even in *icons from Russia*. Sending something through customs with a label that says 'Art Object' certainly beats marking the stuff 'Top Secret.' It's the perfect setup—which is why I'm sure the gallery is our Russian headquarters. And—" I fished in my pocket a second—"*here*'s our Russian spy!" I waved the gallery announcement at Max.

"Alfred Ornstickler?"

"Not him. *Him*. Mr. G., Mr. James Nassur—the one and only."

Max reached over and took the card out of my hand.

"Yup," I said, "he's just the type of man I'd hire if I were head of Russian Intelligence—neat, competent, no trace of any foreign origins—blends right in and . . . ."

"Beck? How do you spell *Russian*?"

"*Russian*? R-u-s-s-i-a-n."

"That's too bad. If he only had an *i*, it would spell *Russian* backward."

"What?"

"Look. *Nassur* is *Russan* spelled backward."

"*Very* interesting."

"You mean it's significant?"

"Yes. Hmmm . . . . It's the sort of teasing that over-confident people do—only, in this case, James Nassur didn't want to be *too* obvious, so he left out the *i*. But if you pronounce them, *Russan* and *Russian* sound almost the same."

Max smiled proudly as I turned back to my notebook and picked up my pen. "All right," I said and headed another page BIG QUESTIONS. "One more list." Max moved closer. I read aloud as I wrote:

"WHAT IS THE MEANING OF WEDNESDAY NIGHT?
WHAT ARE THE DIAGRAMS?
WHO IS MR. X?
WHAT DOES POTTER HAVE TO DO WITH THIS?
WHAT IS IN THE PADLOCKED CELLAR ROOM?

"Anything to add?"

Max scratched his head. "Um . . . How about the Empire State Building?"

"You mean, because it was glued to the diagram? Well, it's certainly worth looking into, but . . . Max, you don't suppose that was a diagram *of* the Empire State Building, do you? I mean, I know it didn't look like a floor plan or anything, but do you think it was a map of a way to get *to* something in the building?"

Max nodded his head, and I added a final question to the bottom of my list:

WHAT HAS THE EMPIRE STATE BUILDING GOT
TO DO WITH ANY OF THIS?

107

---------------→ 30

Since it was approaching bedtime, I followed Max downstairs to bid Mom and Dad good night.

They were both sitting in the living room. My mother had a huge stack of papers on her lap, and she was in the process of artfully obliterating her students' neatly typed pages with masterful strokes of her red pen. My father was reading the *New York Times*. From the look of it, it was Dan's copy.

Max peered around the corner of the paper for attention and then kissed my father good night, as I stood in line and waited my turn. My father, who was preoccupied by the great events of the day, absently grunted, "Good night," and went on with his reading. So much for the patriarch. My mother, on the other hand, was only too glad to set aside her work. She stretched out her arms and hugged us both until my father interrupted our tender vignette.

"Will you look at this! Preposterous!" The manner in which he was shaking the *New York Times* made it impossible to tell whether he was referring to something in it or something on it. I thought I had better go over and have a look. I took the paper and glanced at the spot where his thumb had been. Under a perfect impression of Dan's full set of teeth, it read:

10 PERCENT OF PAEDIATRICIANS IN CITY HELD TO BE INCOMPETENT: BOARD ADVISES REVIEW OF LICENSING PROCEDURES— MATTER WILL BE INVESTIGATED.

"Gee," I said. "They won't investigate you, Dad, will they?"

"What are you talking about?"

I pointed to the article.

"*Here*, this is the article." He motioned at the paper with a skilfully imprecise gesture.

RUSSIANS MIFFED AT EXCLUSION FROM TRADE TALKS: NATIONS MEET TO PLAN TRADE STRATEGIES ON WEDNESDAY. . . .

I began to read it aloud, but my father, in exasperation over my ineptitude, grabbed the paper away. "Not that, *this!*" and he intoned in his melodic bass:

"SECOND U.S. LAUGHING TURKEY COIN FOUND: PREVIOUS SPECIMEN THOUGHT TO BE ONE OF A KIND, POSSIBLY RAREST COIN IN WORLD. NUMISMATISTS ARGUE AUTHEN- TICITY."

"*See?*" said my father huffily and stabbed the paper

109

with an accuracy he had formerly lacked. *"That* is preposterous! The first one was silly; but a second— ridiculous! They're all crazy! It's out-and-out fraud!"

"You don't trust them, do you, Dad?" said Max, the master of understatement.

"No," my father affirmed emphatically. "Not in the least. I don't trust *anyone* any more."

As we walked to the subway, Max fiddled with the brim of his hat, trying to adjust it à la Dick Tracy or something. I tried to imagine Dick Tracy at the age of seven, which reminded me—

"You want it?" I took a lollipop out of my pocket and offered it to Max. I am not very partial to lime.

He eyed it suspiciously. "Where'd you get it?"

"The dentist came to school today for our annual checkups and handed them out."

"He did? I thought dentists were supposed to fix cavities, not give them to you."

Occasionally, Max comes through with a brilliant analysis of a complex issue. "Of course, Max. They're just trying to drum up a little business for next year. You know—if there were no cavities, all the dentists would be out of work." I walked to the trash can and prepared to drop the candy in.

"No, don't do that!" Max shouted. "I was only asking a simple question." And, so saying, my little brother gallantly sacrificed his pearly whites to the dentists of America. Max is a born martyr.

I do not know why Max had not chosen to wax philosophical before—but now he insisted on mumbling around the edges of his lollipop. He carefully explained something which came out as an incomprehensible series of grunts. "You'll have to say that again; all I caught was the 'mmmmm' and 'dmmmmm.'"

Max shoved the lollipop over to his right cheek, curing his speech impediment—although he now looked like a squirrel with a golf ball in its side pouch.

"What I said," said Max, "is Mom and Dad know about everything, don't they?"

"Well, I guess they must know *something*." Mr. X's visit had created a whole new set of problems—and a word of caution seemed to be in order. "Which means that we've got to be very, *very* careful not to let anything slip; if Mom and Dad knew we knew, they might feel compelled to confine us to our rooms to keep us out of trouble. And we wouldn't want *that* to happen, would we?"

"No . . . ," said Max, getting the point, "you've got the only room with a fire escape."

Max, who was really getting into this spy thing, was still chewing on his lollipop—minus the lime part—when we got to Broome Street. He put up the collar of his jacket and blew imaginary smoke rings with his imaginary cigarette. But it was no time for games. Potter was already on his way—we could see him and the shadowy Mr. X down the street—and today, Potter had neither his moustache nor his big black case. I assumed it could only mean one thing—and I was right.

Although Potter's pace slowed to a reverential shuffle as we neared the Two Continents Gallery, he only paused momentarily to watch some burly men unload the Ace Radio and TV Supply van that had been parked in front of the hardware store. For radio supplies, they were bouncing the crates around pretty well. However, Potter soon lost interest in the scene and resumed his journey up West Broadway at a brisk clip.

"You know, Max," I said as I jumped over an abandoned mattress, "Potter's talents are wasted as a spy—he should have been a New York City tour guide."

"Yeah. Well, I'd prefer a guide with shorter legs," Max puffed as he jogged around an old kitchen sink.

He did have a point, but it wasn't until we reached Washington Square Park that Potter's pace really began to cause problems. As we raced along the asphalt

112

paths, Max became so intent on keeping up with Potter that he failed to keep an adequate eye on what was going on around him. I grabbed him roughly by the arm and pulled him out of the way just in time to avoid his being hit by a spinning Frisbee. It buzzed within a half inch of his ear and cracked against a tree a moment later.

"Phew!" Max whirled around. "Thanks, Beck."

We both turned in the direction from which the Frisbee had come, but the Frisbee thrower seemed to have vanished.

"Ah, well," I said. "An N.Y.U. student with poor eyesight."

"Poor eyesight, nothing!" said Max. "I think—" he lowered his voice—"I think someone just tried to kill me!"

"Oh, come on." I looked at Max, but he was deadly serious.

"*Really*—I saw them do that in the movies once—except it was a hat with a steel brim. I'll bet that was no ordinary Frisbee."

I turned toward the tree, but the Frisbee, like the Frisbee thrower before it, had disappeared. Under the circumstances, I felt it might be best not to stand around and debate the issue, and we soon rejoined Potter as he made his way across Waverly Place.

Some while later, Potter turned down East Seventh Street and walked into a small shop. Mr. X padded up to the building and knelt under a window as Max and

I slipped across the street and into the shadow of a huge church. We had a good view. A sign swinging in the breeze said: THE UKRAINIAN SHOP. But the lettering over the door was more specific. It read: SURMA BOOK AND MUSIC CO.

"Wouldn't you know it?" I whispered to Max.

"Wouldn't you know what?"

"Potter's gone to visit the Russians again." Max looked puzzled. "Ukrainian, Max—the Ukraine. It's part of Russia now."

"It is? You sure?"

"Yeah—that fact is courtesy of sixth-grade social studies. You want me to recite their natural resources?"

"Honey . . . ," said Max.

I thought he was being rather patronizing. "Honey, yourself, dear."

"No, *unfiltered* honey." Not only was his reading improving, but his eyes were better than mine. Sure enough, I could just make out the hand-lettered card in the window from which he had garnered that information. There were also embroidered shirts, and books in the window. However, it was too dark inside to see Potter and I could only guess what he was doing —but I thought I had a pretty good idea.

A few minutes later, Potter emerged with a paper bag in his hand and headed west—with Mr. X right behind. Max and I made a slight detour, to get a closer look at the store before following. Our inspection revealed a previously overlooked window display of incredibly beautiful and intricately decorated eggs —"Ukrainian Easter Eggs for sale"—but we still could see almost nothing of the dark interior beyond.

"Creepy," said Max.

"You can sure say that again."

"Creepy!" Max has always been very literal-minded, even for a seven-year-old.

Potter certainly seemed to be making the rounds this afternoon. His next stop? The Strand Book Store—New and Used. It was a huge place.

"Gee, books!" Max whispered as we stepped over the threshold. Potter and Mr. X had already slipped out of sight.

"What'd you expect? Tropical fish?"

"No—but so many! I've never seen so many books in one place before." There were shelves and shelves, from floor to ceiling, of cookbooks, dog books, cat books, travel books—on and on ad infinitum. And somewhere, into one of those categories, Potter had disappeared.

"Let me see," I said. "Which one do you suppose Potter would choose?"

Max suggested we try Model Airplanes, but I vetoed the suggestion.

"Model Trains?"

"How about Mystery?" I said. Actually, I didn't

expect to find Potter there—and he wasn't either—it's just that it seemed to be the category most appropriate to our situation.

"Russia?"

He wasn't there either. However, on the way from Russia to Blueberry Blintzes (i.e., Ethnic Cooking), Max nudged me. "Look!"

I turned around just in time to see Potter as he snapped a book shut and walked down the aisle. Mr. X crawled off a nearby shelf and followed.

"Hmmmm," I said as I stood where Potter had stood, examining a row of books whose bindings were all neatly aligned—all except one. I pulled it down and read the title—*A Survey of Modern Russian Art*—and tried to imagine what sort of secret had been hiding between its pages only moments before.

Of course, Potter did buy a book on the way out in order to camouflage the pickup. And now that he was outside on the sidewalk, he stopped and switched the bag with the book and the brown bag from Surma into one hand, while he tried to get something out of a pocket with the other. But as he did so, the brown paper bag slipped and thudded to the ground.

"Damn!" said Potter loudly. He stamped his foot. "Damn!" At least he'd learned something during his tenure at Harvard. He knelt down and ripped the bag open. Then, after picking up a number of pieces and wrapping them carefully in his pocket handkerchief, he shook his head sadly and continued on his way.

Max and I hurried over to examine the remains. "Well, I'll be!" I said as I pulled back the edges of the torn bag—for what we'd found were scrambled eggs, uncooked. And floating in among the yolks and whites were the unmistakable bits of the beautifully decorated Ukrainian Easter eggs.

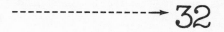

It was somewhere in between the demise of Potter's treasured eggs and our arrival at Astor Place that I began to get this very uneasy feeling—and the goose bumps to match. However, it was Max who articulated the reason.

"Beck, ah . . . don't look now, but, um . . . I think we're being followed."

I stole a hasty look over my shoulder to find a man in a trench coat leaning up against a nearby wall, smoking a cigarette. I had noticed the same man outside Surma and had seen him again at the Strand Bookstore—and I am not *that* much of a believer in coincidence.

"What should we *do*, Max!" I implored in momentary panic.

"Well, ah . . . ."

"Never mind!" I snapped. "We're going to lose him!" And with a firm grip on Max's hand, I took off. The man in the trench coat came right behind: for a big guy, he was pretty darn fast—but we were faster. I did not pause to look back for at least a mile, and when I finally did, our pursuer was nowhere to be seen. "Max . . . ," I panted and tried to catch my breath, "Max, I think we've lost him."

Max was pretty breathless too. "Becky . . . who *was* that guy?"

"I . . . ." I did not get a chance to finish the sentence, for just at that instant, the man in the trench coat stepped up behind me and seized my arm. He reached quickly into his coat. "Oh, my God!" I thought. "Good-bye, Max, good-bye, world!"

A second later, I opened my eyes again—surprised that I *could* open my eyes—to find him waving something in my face as he said clearly, "Officer Martin, Plainclothes, Sixth Precinct." He stopped swishing the thing long enough for me to see that it was a badge with NYPD on it—or, for the uninitiated, the New York Police Department.

"Okay, kids. Game's up. Now tell me where you live and who your parents are."

"Huh? Um . . . officer . . . ," I stalled.

"Gee, we live . . . ." I almost put my whole free hand in Max's mouth.

"We don't live anywhere," I corrected him hastily. "I'm a gypsy—and so's he." I jerked my thumb in Max's direction.

"Yeah, right," Martin countered. "In tennis sneakers and a brand-new goose-down parka—and I'm Whistler's mother. Well, in my opinion, you kids look like a couple of runaways—and it's my job to see that you get back home. Now," he said sternly, "tell me where you live."

I set my jaw firmly and stared at him—the set jaw actually being an attempt to mask my quivering lip. Was this man really a New York City cop? . . . Or was he just pretending to be one? And if he was pretending, what was he going to do with us?

"Won't talk, eh? We'll just see about that." Officer Martin smiled wickedly. "You're both coming with me." And he stood up, taking both my wrist and Max's in one of his hairy, gorilla-like hands. "Now come along."

Under the circumstances, we had very little choice but to follow.

We walked and walked—Max and I and our charming host. Considering Martin's uncertain credentials, it was something of a relief when the Sixth Precinct station house finally came into view. It would have been a

119

pretty stupid place for him to bring his captives if he were *not* a New York City cop. However, we still had two teensy-weensy problems: a) how not to divulge any vital information and b) how to escape. Officer Martin soon simplified things immensely by loosing us from his monstrous grip—I guess he didn't want to look like a child-molester in front of all his cronies. He sat us down on a bench facing the front desk. "Hey, Lou! Keep an eye on these kids for me, will ya? I'm going to check the Missing Persons file . . . and don't you two *move*," he added menacingly before striding off.

"Yeah," Lou seconded and went back to shuffling his papers. But he kept looking up every few seconds to make sure that we hadn't budged.

"Gee," Max said, always thinking of the bright side, "wait until I tell all the kids I've been arrested."

"Don't bother, you haven't been. You're only being detained."

This saddened Max considerably. "Do you think they'll put us in jail?"

"They might—just to keep us out of harm's way. But don't worry, Max, they don't feed prisoners on bread and water any more—nowadays, they throw in a little big of runny gruel." Max huddled closer, and then, leaning forward on the bench, he cocked his head to one side, obviously listening for the sound of cell doors clanging shut.

-----------------→ **33**

We sat there for what seemed to be hours and hours —but according to the clock on the wall, it was only forty-five minutes. It had taken Officer Martin fifteen minutes to research Missing Persons and come up with a blank, fifteen minutes to plead with us and threaten us, and another five to decide to turn the case over to Officer Bockerman, who had ten kids and lived in Brooklyn and was reportedly "very good with children." Officer Bockerman had immediately trooped off to Missing Persons, and he hadn't come back yet. All in all, it was getting rather late.

"Well, Max, it's nice to think that if Mom and Dad get worried enough to call the police and report a kidnapping, the police will already have us. Isn't that convenient? The Law of Supply and Demand: the police have an oversupply of missing children and sooner or later, they will manage to create a demand. It's capitalism in action, a vindication of economic principles . . . oh, never mind." I could tell that sitting around that station house was getting to me. I was almost looking forward to the return of Officer Bockerman.

Meanwhile, Lou was still pushing his pen across the pile of papers and, every so often, answering the phone. It rang again. "Hello. Sixth Precinct. Yes, lady. . . . No. . . ." (I was praying that the "lady" wasn't Mom.) "No lady, cats always seem to get down by themselves. . . . Sure, okay. . . . Why don't you call the Fire Department? . . . Right, good-bye." The phone rang a second time before Lou could even lift his hand from the receiver. "Hello. Sixth Precinct. . . . Oh, Polowski. . . . Yeah. . . . Jeepers! The whole place? You're kidding! . . . No, don't move, hold on. . . . I'll get Mulligan. . . ." He tossed the phone onto the desk and ran out of the room, just like that.

The front hall was empty. The room was empty. I looked at Max. "Come on. Let's get out of here!" And in a flash we were off the bench, out the door, and making tracks for the nearest subway. Free, at last! I didn't think escapes were supposed to be that easy— but I wasn't going to quibble over details.

 34

"Hey, Max. Did you scrub twice?"
"Sure did," Max's voice floated out from the bushes.
I had my doubts, but I dropped the bar of soap into

my book bag anyway. Then I wadded up my disguise and crammed it in on top, realizing as I did so that I wouldn't be needing it any more. One trip to the Sixth Precinct was enough.

Max emerged from the shrubbery. "See?"

I led Max over to the street light to have a good look at him. Double-scrubbed or not, he had the same tell-tale smudges under his eyes. But by now my parents had undoubtedly become so accustomed to seeing those marks that they probably assumed they'd come with the kid. I reached over to flick something off Max's jacket but stopped when I saw that it was a piece of one of Potter's Ukrainian Easter eggs. I picked up the bit of eggshell and examined it.

"Max, did you take any of the pieces of eggshell with you—on purpose?"

"What was left to take? Potter got all the big pieces, and who wants soggy pockets?"

I sighed. "Now we'll never know what they said."

"That's easy," said Max. "They had *butterfingers* written all over them."

"True, but I'll bet those patterns that were painted on the shells had more to say than that. I'm sure Potter had a good reason for taking those pieces— because, as you said, 'who wants soggy pockets?' "

"He put them in a bag," Max corrected.

"Mere technicality. That's pretty good though, isn't it?"

"What?"

"Write a message and then scramble the evidence. It's just too bad that Potter never got as far as the frying pan."

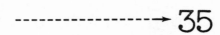 35

The light in the second-floor study was on. I slipped my key into the lock as quietly as I could and prayed that my bat-eared mother would be typing away or doing something equally noisy. Sure enough, not even Dan heard us enter over the furious clacking of the typewriter upstairs. We quickly stowed our gear and went into the kitchen to look for my father, who was not there. I looked in the living room—empty.

"Okay, Max. Just follow me."

With the greatest of stealth, Max and I tiptoed our way to the third floor, where I went into my room, lifted three volumes of the encyclopedia to shoulder height and dropped them onto the floor. Then I slipped into my wooden clogs and raced down the upper flight of stairs, pivoted around the door frame at the entrance to my mother's study, and waited until she looked in our direction.

She regarded us with appropriate surprise. I could tell from the red pinch marks under her glasses that she'd been working a long time. "Where did *you* come from? And where have you *been*! I've been worried sick."

"Upstairs," I said. Whenever possible, I prefer to mislead rather than lie, but sometimes you have to spice it up a bit. "We've been home for at *least* an hour—you were working when we came in and we didn't want to disturb you."

"I see," she said and eyed us doubtfully. "Well, next time, would you mind telling me when you come home anyway? I think I'll probably be able to survive the shock of interruption—after all, this isn't the Gettysburg Address I'm drafting here."

"Sure, Mom," I said cheerily. "By the way, where's Dad?"

"Oh, we'll be eating late," said my mother, looking at her watch and realizing it was already late. "Mrs. Tallucia called to report that her son has appendicitis—last time he swallowed a string of her pearls. Anyway, your father had to go over and keep her from becoming hysterical. He should be back soon."

"Well, I guess I'll go do my homework."

"Yeah," said Max, "and I've got to go finish building my Fokker Triplane."

125

"Don't *you* have any homework?" asked my mother.

"Sure," said Max. "But who's got time for that?"

About fifteen minutes later, the front door opened and all of us—including Dan, who was carrying my father's slippers in his mouth—assembled on the stairs to greet the returning hero, who slammed the door and snarled. "It wasn't appendicitis. Sweet little Joey swallowed the pearls again."

"Again?" said my mother. "Well, didn't Mrs. Tallucia check before she called you? Didn't she know?"

"Of *course* she knew. But that is one very valuable string of pearls—or at least it was. Anyway, Joey's resting comfortably. I wrote him a prescription for some castor oil and I wrote Mrs. Tallucia one for a safe-deposit box, although she may opt for costume jewellery instead. I only hope she doesn't choose any with spikes."

"There, there," said my mother in her most soothing voice. "Dinner's almost ready. Why don't you sit down for a minute and relax? Take off your shoes." She turned to us. "Children—go and wash your hands—please." And she went off into the kitchen. Max and I dutifully ran upstairs, leaving my father and Dan to dispute—with increasingly loud growls on both sides—the ownership of the slippers.

Max was sitting at the recently cleared kitchen table, holding his breath, as he made a fourth attempt to glue a recalcitrant strut on a model of a Fokker Triplane. I watched with interest as the glue stretched and the piece of plastic fell off once more. It is a good thing that Max has not learned to swear yet.

Max sighed, shook up a jar of red paint and prepared to add some detailing to a B–29 Superfortress which had been resting mid-table alongside a newly opened box containing the parts for a Sopwith Camel.

"Why don't you just finish the Triplane, Max? It might be easier if you stuck to one thing."

"Beck, please." Max glared at me with the expression he reserves for meddling dilettantes and dabbed a red speck on the B–29.

"You don't understand—it's the challenge of the thing."

"Sure," I said—who was I to argue with such ardour?

Meanwhile, back at the sink, Mom and Dad, who had excused us from dish duty, hung up their matching dish towels. Then my mother wandered over to inspect the work of her third offspring, pausing en route to shoo a loudly meowing Armenia away from the refrigerator.

"How nice!" she cooed and peered over Max's shoulder. The adoring public was beginning to rattle the maestro. He dropped his brush, which smeared a red blob of paint across the wing of the B–29. Max gave Mom a dirty look.

"It's all right," she said. "I was just leaving. Besides, I think I hear the telephone about to ring." A second later, it did—I don't know *how* she does that.

"Hello? Oh, hello, Arthur! . . ." She paused a moment, suddenly aware that all eyes in the room were upon her. "Hold on a minute, Arthur. I think I'll take this call in my study." She held out the phone to me. "Be a dear and hang up when I pick up on the other end, will you?"

"I will." And I did—I know enough not to try and listen in on my mother's conversations.

When I got back to the table, Max was scrubbing away at the blob of paint with a rag and paint remover. From the look of things, it was removing the wing as well.

"Hey, why do you think she changed phones like that?" Max said and moistened his rag again.

"Well, maybe she's discussing something she doesn't want us to hear." Talk about stating the obvious.

"But that's not like her," Max fretted. "It isn't *normal*."

"Max, dear, there isn't much that *is* normal around here any more—or hadn't you noticed?"

------------------→ 37

Sometimes Max really is a wonder. I watched as he applied the finishing touches of blue paint to the Fokker and set his brush down. To his right stood a completed B–29 and on his left, a half-finished Sopwith Camel. Not bad.

"Pretty good, huh, Beck?" Max smiled with satisfaction—he has never been one for false modesty.

"Yup," I said, "considering that you . . . ." But Max was not listening to me any more. He had shifted his attention to Armenia, who was pacing rapidly in front of the refrigerator, stopping every once in a while to paw at the door.

Max walked over, carefully opened the door, and peered in—but his head re-emerged a split second later. "Yikes! A fish!" He slammed the door shut. Armenia barely escaped with her life.

I had visions of a glassy-eyed, twenty-pound bass, but examination revealed that it was both less than twenty pounds and less than a bass. Quite a treat for the old olfactory membranes: it seems that my mother, as is her custom on occasion, had bought a fish for Armenia; and, as is also her custom, had wrapped it up in a copy of the *New York Times*—*without* a plastic bag.

Armenia, sensing that the time was ripe (as well as the fish), leaped into the re-opened icebox, while Max, who is a great believer in theatrics, stood by, holding his nose. It was obviously up to me to do something—luckily, I am great in emergencies. I quickly evicted our presumptuous feline and took possession of the package.

"Hey, Max, hold Armenia!"—who was at that moment trying to climb up to the fish by the shortest route possible, i.e., my leg—"I can't do everything."

Max let go of his nose and collared the cat.

As I set the package down on the counter, I noticed an intriguing headline framed within the fish's gaping jaws.

"Hey, Max! Come here—look at this."

RUSSIANS MIFFED AT EXCLUSION FROM
TRADE TALKS: NATIONS MEET TO PLAN
TRADE STRATEGIES ON WEDNESDAY.

"Interesting—yes? It's got our two clues in it."

"Wow!" I could not tell whether this was a reaction to our new discovery, or whether Armenia had just dug her claws into Max's shoulder. "Haven't I heard that somewhere before?" he added.

"Well, aren't you glad you're hearing it again? Now . . . if I can just find the rest of the article. . . ." I lifted a floppy fish fin. "Here it is," and I began to read:

130

"The U.S. and major European nations are planning to meet in New York City next week to map strategies for cooperation in international trade for the coming years. The talks, which will open Wednesday evening at the Waldorf, are considered to be of major importance and may have far-reaching consequences concerning the economic patterns of global trade over the next decade."

I moved another fin.

"A spokesman for the conference said that due to the Soviet persecution of the dissident scholar Alexi Montorovoff, eleven nations had voted to exclude the Russian delegation from the talks. However, the Russians, who have not softened their position on Mr. Montorovoff, have made it plain that they consider this punitive action to be unwarranted interference and have warned that without their presence, the meeting may be a terrible fiasco. 'After all,' their spokesman said, 'it seems foolhardy to conduct the meeting in an atmosphere of top-secret exclusivity—the goods of too many nations are involved and we believe these talks should not be closed to us.' He added, 'We are all playing for very high stakes: trade is power.'"

I replaced the fish tail and looked at Max. "You know, I'm beginning to get this feeling of déjà vu."

"Does that mean you're going to be sick?"

"No, Max. Déjà vu means that you've seen something before—or heard it before. . . ."

131

"You mean, like re-reading the article you started to read yesterday?"

"Well, yes. Except there's something more to this. There are key words like *unwarranted interference, high stakes, terrible fiasco, top secret. . . .*"

"They sound like bits of Potter's conversations."

"Good thinking, Max." I scanned the page again. "Hmmmm. This definitely warrants further investigation . . . just as soon as I get rid of *this*." So saying, I rolled the *Times* back around the fish, tied it tightly in a plastic bag, and threw the whole thing back in the fridge.

Max pulled the most recent *New York Times* out of a pile of papers and handed it to me. Today's news flash item was on the opening of model sailboat season in Central Park, and then there were a few notes about a heat wave in Moscow. Conveniently, the *Times* had grouped its Russian stories.

RUSSIAN DELEGATION STILL BARRED FROM TRADE TALKS: ANGER MOUNTS ON BOTH SIDES

A spokesman for the eleven nations that are to meet Wednesday said that the conference, "which will concern very delicate matters," will start on schedule despite a Russian assertion that decisions made without their presence will be meaningless.

Mr. Charonski, speaking for the Russians, called the exclusion "from such important talks" an "outrage." Mr. Charonski was asked if, under the circumstances, the U.S.S.R. would make any move to disrupt the conference. "Certainly not," Mr. Charonski said. "We thoroughly disapprove of the decision—but we are not barbarians." Moscow will continue to protest the action.

I sat down and stared at the paper as Max bit his fingernail and tried to be patient. He didn't try very long. "It's just the same stuff about the talks as yesterday, isn't it?"

"Except that part about the possibility of disruption," I corrected.

"What disruption? Didn't the Russians say they weren't going to disrupt the talks?"

"Yes, Max," I sighed impatiently. "That's what they *said*, but saying something doesn't make it true."

 38

We walked into the kitchen the following morning and found my father already seated at the table. He looked up from reading the *New England Journal of Medicine.* "*Buon giorno!* . . . My, don't we look wide awake this morning!" He flashed us a saccharine smile.

I glared at him. A moment later, my mother fairly danced into the kitchen in an equally obnoxious good mood. She was suspiciously well-dressed for her usual Saturday slouching around. Then, without asking our opinions on the matter, she started dropping frozen pancakes into the toaster—which is a relatively disgusting food and something she only serves when she either a) bears someone a terrible grudge or b) is in a hurry. And since I could not remember any stormy scenes from the night before, I deduced that she was in a rush—even though she was now carefully and patiently boning Armenia's fish. I began to wonder, if she really had it to do all over again, whether she would trade Max and me in for two more cats.

However, such thoughts were interrupted by a horrible mechanical gurgle from the toaster, which indicated that our pancakes had gotten caught midway through popping up. My mother quickly unplugged the contraption and, using a fork, fished out the contents. She brought over the remains.

"They broke a little getting them out," she said, trying to absolve herself of any guilt. "But they'll taste just the same." On which point, she happened to be correct. Rotten is rotten. However, maple syrup is not bad. I decided to see if the lovely specimens I had

134

before me would float. Max apparently had the same idea.

"Well," said my mother, lovingly stroking Armenia's back as the cat wolfed down *its* breakfast, "try not to dawdle this morning—I'd like to beat the crowds to Bloomingdale's."

"Bloomingdale's!" I said as a piece of pancake slid off my fork and plopped back into the syrup. The implication was that she was not going alone.

"Bloomingdale's," my mother repeated. Now Bloomingdale's is a rather unmanageable store any day of the week, but on Saturday, it is a veritable madhouse and one would need a pretty good reason to willingly subject oneself to that sort of pandemonium. Clearly, my mother felt that she had adequate reasons. She held up a blue denim rag. *"These* are a disgrace. . . . I found them in the hamper this morning. *Obviously,* Max needs something to wear." I guessed at that point that the aforementioned rag had, until this morning, passed for Max's blue jeans. She chucked them into the wastebasket. Max gasped.

Then my mother proceeded to state's exhibit number two. "This is, likewise, a sorry piece of attire," she said and picked up Max's jacket—which looked a little bit less chic in the morning light. "As a matter of fact, after checking Max's closets, I have come to the conclusion that he has very little to wear." She leaned over the back of my chair. And then, considering that she was right next to my ear, she finished rather loudly: "Oh, yes . . . and I forgot to mention the fact that I need to replace all my make-up, which has some-how"—and she hung on the word—"*mysteriously* dis-appeared—I just can't imagine *where* it goes."

 **39**

"Max, that's revolting." Max had just managed, while applying a smidgen of toothpaste to his toothbrush, to spray the whole mirror with the stuff. "Besides, you're hogging the sink." I rinsed out my brush and hung it up. Max continued to polish his incisors.

I waited a moment and then asked in a more affec-tionate voice, "How would you feel if I didn't go with you and Mom?"

The look on Max's face told me immediately how he felt. "B-Beck!" he said while swallowing a mouthful of toothpaste. "You can't go off after Potter without me!"

"Shhh! You want the whole East Side to know?" I handed him the water glass. "All right, all right. I just thought I'd ask—I hope you're aware that we may be wasting valuable time by all this."

"If I have to go, you have to go," said Max, fully convinced that he had Justice on his side.

And so I went—I am nothing if not a loyal sister.

Of course, my mother was also well aware that my presence on this expedition was extraneous, but a trip to Bloomingdale's is about as close as we ever get to a family outing. . . . My father managed to have himself excused from all this joyous togetherness on the grounds that he was saving the world from a case of swollen glands. In spite of his defection, my mother remained in a rather festive mood; we were going "downtown," as she called it.

Max and I clumped after her, through the front door and down the steps.

"Can I do it?" I asked, preparing to raise my arm and display my new-found skill at hailing a cab.

"Can you do what?" she asked innocently.

"Hail a cab," I answered impatiently.

"You probably *can*," she said, "but you *may* not." A case of advanced semantics. And then she added, "We're going to walk."

"Walk! But it's almost two miles!" One of the less well-known facts about my mother is that she is a sporadic exercise freak.

"Yes, walk. It's too nice a day not to."

"It's too nice a day to spend in Bloomingdale's," I returned.

"How did I ever have such spoiled children?" she said and raised her eyes skyward. And then, without waiting for an answer, she set off—happily striding in time to the tune of "Waltzing Matilda," which she was singing in a loud, clear, and tuneful soprano.

 40

Sometimes, Max and I try to pretend that we don't know her; for instance, when she starts skipping down the street, or calling "Glorious day!" to anyone who happens to be passing by. Who else's mother acts like that? My class once took a vote, and I was chosen "kid with the weirdest mother."

This trip was less eventful than most. She scared the postman half to death by jumping up from the other side of the mailbox—something which she later swore she had not done on purpose: she'd actually been hunting for a penny she had dropped—which in itself is pretty odd, considering that, with inflation and all, even *Max* doesn't chase after pennies any more.

That and a few other minor incidents notwithstanding, we arrived at Bloomingdale's at a respectable hour —only to find that half of New York had gotten up earlier.

"Well, where shall we go first?" my mother asked

brightly as a huge woman lunged past her to get at a stack of pocketbooks which were on sale. After almost being clipped behind the ear by a brown bag, Mom decided that almost any place had to be better than where she was standing and we made our way through the crowds, over to Cosmetics. Mom found a saleslady, and samples of eye-shadow were soon spread out before her in all their multicoloured glory. My mother turned to me. "How do you like this one?"

"Well, frankly, I think it's ghastly."

"Good," she said and held the cake out to the saleslady. "I'll take two of these." She also bought eye-liner, eyebrow pencil, and some other stuff before turning her saleslady over to the next person in line—a peculiar little woman who had spent the last five minutes telling me about her Martian friends and how they'd taught her needlepoint.

Now we were ready for the pièce de résistance: Max's wardrobe. "All right, where have they put the escalators?" my mother asked, implying that some enterprising gremlins had moved them while she had had her back turned. "Oh. Here they are!" and we all clambered onto the escalator—right behind the man in the long black cape and the big black hat. I held my breath momentarily, but of course, it turned out to be neither Potter nor Mr. X. I guess that spy outfits must be pretty big this year.

When we reached the Boys' Department on the

second floor, we found it filled with a noisy assortment of other people's little brothers. Mom elbowed her way in and walked over to a rack of suits and blazers. Max instinctively backed away.

"We'd like some blue jeans, please," she said to the gentleman she had cornered against the wall. Max breathed a sigh of relief.

The salesman peered at Max over the edge of his bifocals and smiled condescendingly. "Are you sure you don't want *that* department?" he asked and nodded toward the little boys' alcove.

"*Yes!*" said Max with a trifle more emphasis than was necessary.

"He's small for his age," my mother added helpfully. "He's seven." And I noticed that Max was trying, as unobtrusively as possible, to stand on tiptoe.

"Heavens! I would have guessed *five*," exclaimed the dean of tact. "Oh, well. Appearances *are* deceptive," and he patted Max on the head. "Now, blue jeans you said?"

"Yes, please."

"What colour?"

"Blue jeans are usually blue," said my mother, the stickler—but the gentleman for whom this clarification was intended had already trotted off to see what was in stock. Luckily, Max is a sort of average, all-around, small blue-jean size, and it did not take long to find him a suitable pair.

"What next?" my mother asked no one in particular. "Oh, yes. A jacket." She started looking through a nearby rack. "How about this?" she asked and held one up.

"How . . . ." Max hesitated. ". . . how about a trench coat?" The inflection at the end of his sentence clearly indicated that he did not expect to get one.

My mother turned around and gave Max a funny look.

". . . with epaulettes?" he added weakly.

Then I gave him a stern look.

". . . that will be fine," he finished.

Actually, the arms on the jacket made him look like a chimpanzee. So after a few more unflattering experiments, Max finally settled for a utilitarian, all-purpose blue windbreaker, which was followed in quick succession by a green sweater, two shirts, a pair of "good" slacks, and five pairs of socks.

"Have I forgotten anything?" my mother pondered aloud and swung almost full circle, stopping as she eyed a case she had previously overlooked. "Underwear!" she called as though greeting a long-lost friend. "How silly of me to forget!" Max, who had turned bright red, was starting to edge away. Second-graders are very sensitive.

"It's all right, Max," I said comfortingly. "*Everyone* wears underwear," and then, feeling that perhaps I had overstated the case, "well, almost." It took Mom quite a while to finish the conversation she was having with the salesman about the effects of elastic waistbands on the circulation of the blood, but she finally did—and the colour of Max's face changed from vermillion back to its usual healthy blush.

Then, not wanting to overstay our welcome, my mother had all the items totalled up, dumped into a shopping bag, and paid for with one flash of her magic credit card; she hardly ever deals in the realm of plain green money like ordinary mortals.

------------------→ 41

"Well, what shall we do this afternoon?" asked my mother, who had just treated us to a lovely junk food lunch. The way she phrased the question seemed to hint that whatever we did, she was going to do it too.

"Perhaps you'd like to skulk around dark corners on Broome Street," I said.

"What?"

"Nothing."

"How about the Metropolitan Museum?"

"Naw. . . ."

"The Guggenheim?"

"Oh, Mom. . . ."

"The United Nations?"

"Uh-uh."

She sighed in resignation. "That's the trouble with you two party-poopers. We live right here in New York City and we never get to see half as much of it as the tourists do." (I don't suppose it would have occurred to her to see it without us.) "When was the last time you went to the Museum of Natural History or Saint Patrick's Cathedral or Rockefeller Center, the Statue of Liberty, the Empire State Building . . . ?"

"How *about* the Empire State Building?" I interrupted, realizing that we might be able to combine a little business with pleasure.

"*What* about the Empire State Building?" asked my mother.

"Can we go?"

"Well, I actually had something a little more cultural in mind, but . . . oh, why not? It might be fun."

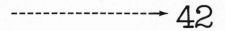 42

"Wow!" I said as I stepped out onto the observation deck of the Empire State Building. "Will you look at that!" Even to a jaded New Yorker like me, the view from the 86th floor was spectacular.

143

"Wow!" said Max, looking down. Very original.

My mother moved to the eastern wall, where she stood for a few minutes, gazing intently at the traffic patterns on Fifth Avenue, before adding her two cents. "Do you realize how many cabs there are in this city?" She motioned for us to come look at the yellow traffic jam below. "Amazing!"

"You want to hear something even more amazing?" Max said and tried to hold our complimentary information folder steady against the breeze. "'Facts About the Empire State Building,'" he read. "'Snow and rain can be seen falling up! Rain is sometimes red!'"

"Really?"

"Yeah! It says so right here," and Max continued, ". . . 'ships can be seen forty miles at sea' . . . and you can give someone 'shocking kisses, due to at-at-at. . . .'"

"'Atmospheric conditions,'" I read, coming to his rescue.

Mom thought this last one was particularly interesting and we spent the next two minutes ducking and sidestepping as she tried to test the truth of the statement.

"You know, you two are no fun at all!" she said finally and walked off, undoubtedly looking for some other poor, unsuspecting soul to kiss.

I waited for my mother to disappear around the

corner before changing the subject. "Okay, Max. Time for work."

"Right, Beck." He refolded his booklet.

"We've got to find out what's important about this building—or rather, what's important to Mr. G, Mr. X, and Potter."

"Right, Beck."

"I suppose the observation deck is as good a place to start as any."

"Right, Beck."

I looked at Max. It makes me very uneasy when people agree too readily. "And stop saying, 'Right, Beck.'"

"Okay, Beck. Beck?"

"Yes?"

"Where in the heck do we start?"

"Start?" I echoed sarcastically. "I know we don't have the faintest idea what we're looking for, but what makes you think we're going to have any problems?"

"I didn't say we would," Max answered doubtfully.

"Good. Then let's get down to work."

What I discovered during my perambulation was a pretty ordinary observation deck—and nothing more. I found Max again where we'd started. I looked at him hopefully. "Any luck?"

He displayed his empty hands and shrugged. "You?"

"Me neither," I sighed. "Max, I get this terrible feel-

145

ing that we are missing the point. It doesn't make sense
—why would anyone hide anything up here? It's not
very convenient and not very accessible and there are
too many people walking around. If you had the whole
city of New York in which to hide something, would
you hide it up here?"

"Uh-uh," Max said. He began rolling and unrolling
his information folder absently.

"And for the same reasons, it's not the best spot in
New York for a secret rendezvous either."

"But what if whatever-it-is is somewhere else in the
building?"

"Even if it is, there still has to be some very good
reason for choosing this building above any other—
there has to be something here which no other building has: something intrinsic, something immov-
able. . . ."

"Is it the view? Are they watching something?"

"Maybe. But there are other views in New York,
and there are helicopters and satellites and hot-air
balloons. . . . What *is* so unique about this pile of
bricks!" In exasperation, I looked around the deck
again. . . . "Max, stop that! Of course!"

"Stop what?"

"Stop playing with that folder—and give it to me."

"Huh?" He handed it over obediently.

"For the past half hour, while we've been running

around trying to figure this thing out, you've been holding this silly folder—which just happens to contain a list of *everything* that's special about this building."

"I have?" said Max, unsure whether to congratulate himself or apologize. "It's not red rain or shocking kisses; is it?"

"No. I think it's pretty safe to rule those out. Let me see. . . . 'There are 6,500 windows' in the building and '60,000 tons of steel; enough to build a double-track railroad from New York to Baltimore.'"

I paused to ponder that one: a giant electromagnet? "'1,860 steps on the stairs. 60 miles of water pipe, a master FM antenna . . . and above the 102nd floor . . . is a 222-foot, 70-ton structure. . . .'" I began to get this prickly feeling all up and down my spine. "'It is the world's most powerful and far-reaching television antenna structure . . . used by all TV stations in the metropolitan area, including UHF and VHF stations. It reaches 8,000,000 sets in a four-state area.'"

"Max," I said and shook his hand, "Max, old buddy, we've got it!"

---------------→ 43

I handed my mother another quarter (pay binoculars do not take credit cards) and followed Max, who was impatiently waiting for me to finish my explanation. We moved down the platform, out of earshot.

"Okay, Max. The key word is *disrupt*; the Russians are going to try to disrupt the Wednesday trade talks."

"But why?"

"Well, in the first place, if they arrange a really good disruption, the meeting will be postponed—and so will any unfavourable trade agreements. And secondly, by the time the meeting reconvenes, the whole Montorovoff affair may have blown over. Then the Russians would be allowed to participate—and that's something they desperately want to do. Like the man said, Max, 'Trade is power.'"

Max nodded his head knowingly.

"However, the Russians have a problem because they have the best motive for disrupting the conference and they'll immediately be suspect. They've got to make it look as if someone else is responsible, and that's why the whole thing will be done indirectly, as a byproduct of a far greater disturbance."

"A greater disturbance? Like what?"

"Oh, not much—just a little something like creating utter chaos in the whole metropolitan area; a simple thing, if they control *that* transmission tower and can broadcast from it." I pointed above us. "Figure two people per TV set, eight million sets, not to mention the FM radio stations. . . . . They can get a lot of attention that way, and with proper planning, they should be able to create enough fear, suspicion, and confusion to last the city for weeks."

"Gosh!" Max shook his head. "But what are they going to put on TV?"

"Well, it won't be reruns of 'Marvin the Mighty Man.' Undoubtedly, it will be something designed to throw everyone off their tracks—like claiming to be some sort of radical fringe and then spouting the propaganda to match."

"And the conference will be stopped because everyone in the city will be scared?"

"Brilliant deduction, Max. It won't exactly be the sort of atmosphere in which foreign diplomats will want to sit down and work out intricate trade policies —at least that's what the Russians are hoping. . . . So," I concluded, "does it all make sense to you now?"

"Yes," said Max soberly. "It sure does. . . . It's kind of frightening, isn't it, Beck?"

"Yes, it is," I agreed. "But we haven't got time to

149

be scared." I started to move back to where Mom was waving her arms and motioning for us to come have a look, but Max caught my sleeve.

"Beck?"

"Yes?"

"There's just one thing. You didn't say how the Russians were going to take over the TV tower."

"Oh . . . well, that's the part I haven't figured out yet."

 44

Max, in an obvious play for sympathy, was doing a lot of huffing and puffing, and grunting and groaning as he lugged his bicycle up from the basement. It was a waste of dramatic talent, since I rarely fall for that sort of thing—and besides, I had my own bicycle to carry.

"Look, Max. It's very simple. Either we ride, or we don't go downtown." A very expensive plate of blueberry blintzes and a week's worth of subway riding had just about exhausted my meagre financial resources —but at least Sunday is allowance day, so there was help on the way—later. For now, a little muscle power would have to do; I tried to ignore the sorrowful moan behind me as Max hoisted his cycle up another step.

When we were out on the sidewalk, I took the two brown paper bags containing the gourmet picnic, thoughtfully provided by my mother, and strapped them onto the carrier of my bike. Ostensibly, Max and I were on our way over to Central Park for a day of riding on its traffic-free roads and paths—with explicit instructions to ride our bikes on the sidewalk and walk them across intersections until we got there. I would never dream of questioning parental authority—so I waited until we were safely out of sight of my mother's study window before nosing my bike down the kerb and onto the street.

Max hesitated. "Beck," said the Voice of Reason, "Mom and Dad will kill us if they find out we've been riding on the street."

"They may not get the pleasure," I said and smiled as a taxi swerved over in my direction, within two centimetres of my left toe, and then roared away. "In which case," I added cheerfully, "I'm leaving you my set of darts, my quilted bedspread, my baseball glove, my Peter Frampton albums. . . ."

Max, realizing that he was onto a good thing, followed me into the street.

Everything considered, the ride downtown wasn't too bad. We did ride on the sidewalks between 57th Street and 34th Street, where the traffic was particularly heavy, but other than that, we took our chances with the cabs and potholes. It was smooth sailing until down around Houston Street, which is where the Highway Department had given up and where the cobbled streets began: it was then that I understood why they'd nicknamed the early bicycles "bone-shakers."

But in spite of all the bumps (and bruises), Max and I soon found ourselves riding past the Two Continents Gallery. The blinds in the gallery windows were drawn shut this sleepy morning—unlike those in the hardware store, where a band of industrious folks were up and about, unloading another Ace Radio and TV truck and bouncing electrical components around with their customary vigour.

"Hey, it's Sunday," said Max, "and they're working."

"So are we," I reminded him and pedalled on.

A few minutes later, we arrived at Broome Street and settled into our usual dark entranceway (after checking the adjacent doorways for signs of Mr. X and finding none). That was the exciting part. Then, for an hour, we sat. I taught Max how to play Geography and Dictionary, but eventually even they could not help to pass the time.

"Supposing he's not home," Max sighed at last. "We could wait here all day for nothing . . . ," and then, reconsidering, "unless he's still asleep."

152

But it was fairly late—and even on Sundays, Potter had never been a late sleeper. I looked at Max, who was already on his feet. "Well, I suppose the only thing to do in a situation like this is to poke around a little. . . ." Max poked me in the ribs a few times and I restrained my urge to strangle him. I grabbed his hand instead. "—like listening at his door to see if we can hear any signs of movement on the other side."

"Good," said Max. "Let's go."

Max led the way across the street and held the door open for me, like a young gentleman. Generally, I do not approve of such anachronisms, but I did feel that as the older sibling, I should lead the way up the stairs—just in case danger was lurking around the corner. I did not get the chance to see what was lurking around the corner, however.

"Beck!" Max hissed. "Look!" When I turned around, I found Max still at the bottom of the stairs, pointing to a white piece of paper that was sticking out of one of the mailboxes. Potter's box.

"Should we open it?" Max asked.

Even I am smart enough to know that tampering with the U.S. Mail constitutes a federal offence. But first of all, it wasn't all the way *in* the mailbox; second, it didn't look as though it had actually been *mailed;* and third, it would be *very* easy to open. It was just a piece of folded paper.

"Of course."

Max gingerly extracted the message and handed it to me. I opened it and read:

"Saturday

"Doug,

"Gone up north—be back Wednesday. Want to clear up all my affairs. Pray for government intervention. See you Wednesday. 7:30. Two Continents.

"W.P.C."

I glanced over the sheet again and then refolded it carefully. At least now we knew the time for Wednesday's "event." But what was "Want to clear up all my affairs" supposed to mean? And what about "Pray for government intervention"? Whose government? Our government? Armed intervention? As I mulled over the possibilities, I came to only one conclusion: hanging around Broome Street, with Potter gone, wasn't going to help us find any answers.

→ 45

"Well, what will it be?" I said to Max as we wheeled our bikes up the path in Central Park. "We could picnic there, near Balto." I nodded at the statue of the courageous dog who had delivered serum to Nome, Alaska, during the 1925 diphtheria epidemic.

"Nah, it would be too much like having Dan drool over your shoulder. It could make you lose your appetite."

"In your case, I'd say that would be highly unlikely. . . . How about the boat pond at Seventy-second Street?" I was referring to the cement-walled pool where New York City sails its model boats.

"Okay," Max said enthusiastically, in the belief that a model anything had to be better than a bronze anyone. "Let's go there."

We took the long way around, past the Alice in Wonderland statue, and thudded our way down the steps and onto the terrace that surrounds the pond. At the moment, an elderly gentleman was using a stick to push his pint-sized Spanish galleon away from the wall, while a number of sleek sloops were heeling midwater in a mini-regatta. I disentangled our lunch from my bike carrier and we sat down on a nearby bench.

"I'm *starved*," said Max as he took one of the brown paper bags. "I sure hope it's *good*."

That, of course, would depend on how much inspiration our mother had used in filling the sandwiches—the less, the better. I never minded the tuna fish and pickle sandwiches, or the ham, cheese, and orange slices; but I was not a big fan of the cream cheese and walnut, or the peanut butter, banana, and bacon.

"What've you got?" Max asked.

I cautiously lifted my bread, which was plain old white bread—unquestionably employed to lull the eater into a false sense of security. "Roast beef, apples, and mayonnaise." It could have been worse. I breathed a sigh of relief.

"Want to trade?"

I would've had to have been a fool to agree to the transaction without knowing all the facts. "What have you got?"

"It doesn't look bad. . . . It's sort of cream cheese, pimiento, and knockwurst—I think."

"Sorry, Max. You know I'm allergic to pimientos."

"You are?"

I bit into my sandwich, which settled the matter, and snapped the pop-top off my can of lukewarm Coke.

Max, having resigned himself to his fate, seemed to thoroughly enjoy his lunch—if speed is any indication. "What are we supposed to do now?" he asked as he

156

licked the final bits of cream cheese off his fingers.

"Eat your apple."

"No, I mean, what are we supposed to do about Potter and everything?"

"Oh, that," I said and tossed a few crusts of bread at the pigeons. "Well, since we can't tail Potter all over creation any more—due to the fact that the tailee has skipped town—I think it might be a good time to do a little investigative research."

"Investigative research?" Max repeated. "Are we going to break into Potter's apartment and search it?" My innocent little brother was rapidly developing a devious cast of mind.

"That might turn up a lot of information, but it might also land us in jail—or get us *shot* by the CIA. I'm sure they have the place under some kind of surveillance."

"Oh," said Max, crestfallen.

"Actually, I had something a little less illegal in mind; such as doing some real research on TV transmitters and telecommunications and digging up some more background on the trade talks. Which means we'll need a few good books and copies of the *New York Times* for the last couple of weeks."

"But, Beck, you know what happens to old *New York Timeses*." Max held his nose in memory of Armenia's breakfast.

157

"I know what happens to them in *our* house—that's why we're going to the New York Public Library."

 46

The next afternoon, Max and I walked down Fifth Avenue, hand in hand, in the direction of the library. In front of us, the Empire State Building loomed against the sky, a constant reminder of our mission. Too constant. Max had become fixated on the subject.

". . . so you think a whole bunch of Russians are going to attack the Empire State Building?"

Television is a pernicious influence. "Max, I didn't say that, you did. And in any case, I don't think it— New York may not be the most civilized city in the world, but it's definitely not the least either. I think whatever they do here, they'll do it with a little flare."

"Bombs?"

"*No*, Max—suavity, subtlety, finesse. . . ."

"How about slipping sodium pentothal into the water coolers and drugging all the guards?"

This conversation was mercifully interrupted by our arrival at the New York Public Library on 42nd Street. For a moment, we stood gazing up at the magnificent stone lions outside: the imposing guardians of the Gates of Knowledge, one of which had a pigeon on its head. Then Max and I walked up the wide steps slowly, with all the reverence due such a great shrine.

"What'd they do with all the books?" Max whispered as he stepped out of the revolving door and looked around at the huge and basically empty main lobby. Quite a change from the Book Nook at school.

"It's just the entrance hall; they've got the books around here—someplace."

With my steps echoing on the marble floor, I walked across to a lone gentleman standing at the Inquiry Desk. He was reading a newspaper that drooped gracefully over the front of the counter.

I cleared my throat. "Excuse me, sir?"

He peered up at me through his gold-rimmed pince-nez. "Yes?"

"Where can I find books on television—I mean," I corrected myself hastily, "telecommunications." This was obviously not the sort of place in which one mentioned the boob tube out loud—unless he or she were also fond of swearing in church.

"Ah! Telecommunications!" he said as if he had recently been deluged with inquiries on the subject. "You'll have to look that up in the Main Catalogue, Room 315." He nodded to his left and went back to reading his paper.

Following in the general direction of his nod soon brought us to the elevators, and with a quick push of the old button, we were on our way to the third floor. Room 315 turned out to be a place the size of Radio City Music Hall, where thousands of file drawers arranged in alphabetical order lined the walls and snuggled into polished wooden cabinets. I found "T" on my left; "T" for "television." There were three full drawers on the subject; say, six thousand cards or so, each one representing a book—this was clearly not the place for casual browsers.

I sighed loudly and started flipping through the cards, looking first for "Television transmitters," then "Television antennas," and a whole lot of other categories that the New York Public Library had not deigned to list. It was about half an hour later that I discovered some spiteful soul had hidden the information I wanted under "Television: relay systems." There were lots of books on the topic. I decided to pick cards for the first four.

Which brought me to another problem: how to get a book.

Matters were simplified by an explanation from a blue-jeaned, work-booted young man who was reading through a file drawer a little way down the line. Actually, the procedure was not difficult—even if it wasn't your normal, run-of-the-mill library routine.

Basically, you were supposed to fill out a "call slip" with the book's number and drop it in a box and then wait for the book to be brought to you in the Reading Room, which was straight through Room 315. Simple enough—that is, *if* you can get someone to accept your call slips.

We walked over to the desk. "I'd like to put these in to get books, please," I said and held out my slips.

The lady at the desk looked up. "Ah, this is an adult research library, you know." (I didn't.) "Why don't you try the children's room at the Donnell?"

"At the Donnell? On Fifty-third Street? But . . . uh . . . um . . . we can't." And then I added, pointing at Max, "He's much too smart for children's books." Secretly, I just hoped he'd be smart enough to keep quiet.

"He is?" She looked at Max.

"Yes," I said, and on the theory that a big lie wouldn't do any more harm than a little one, I continued, "As a matter of fact, this young man happens to be a certified child prodigy, and he *only* reads adult books—he hasn't touched the other stuff since he was three." Max stood there, shifting his weight uneasily from foot to foot and sniffling. I handed him a Kleenex and continued. "He's a real, bona fide genius, another Newton, another Einstein. . . ."

"Yeah," Max interrupted, "E=mc²"—which is a nice

equation, even though I'm positive Max didn't have the vaguest idea what it meant.

She leaned forward and scrutinized Max carefully as he tried to look his most intelligent. "Hmmmmm . . . well, all right. This time, but . . . ."

"Oh, thank you!" I said and shoved the call slips into her hand before she could change her mind. Then we hurried away from the desk. But the lady continued to stare after us—undoubtedly wondering why this extraordinary marvel of human intelligence looked like such a thoroughly ordinary seven-year-old kid.

Max and I walked through the wide doorway at the other end of Room 315 and into the Reading Room, where, after a fifteen-minute wait, we collected our books. I carried our materials over to one of the mammoth tables and put the books down—a little loudly, if one were to judge by the reaction of fifty nearby scholars who turned in our direction and scowled.

I picked up a volume. *Television Relay Systems Modification Specifications of Frequency-Voltage Input-Output Operating Ratios*. It looked promising.

It took only a few minutes of concentrated effort to prove that it was not: that's how long it took me to figure out what the title meant. I thought I'd better try another one and reached for an innocuous-looking little tome entitled *Recent Evaluative Studies of An-*

tenna Transmission Devices in Multidimensional Wide-Range Telecommunications. I opened it up and stared at a few diagrams. They bore an interesting resemblance to some of Potter's diagrams—and were equally enigmatic. I couldn't make heads or tails of them. In fact, I soon discovered I was holding the book upside down—a confirmation of my growing suspicion that we were getting nowhere. That, coupled with a certain dizziness, encouraged me to reassess our course of action.

"Uh . . . Max . . . I've been doing some serious thinking about children's books. . . ."

"You mean you can't read these?" Max interrupted.

"That's not the point, dear. It's just that I'm beginning to think that children's books may be a little better suited to our purposes: a little more concise, a little less technical. I wouldn't have to wade through so much extraneous . . . ."

"I knew it. You can't read them."

"Let's *not* get personal," I said, and led the way out of the room.

I figured it would take us about fifteen minutes to walk up to the Donnell—but then, I hadn't planned on any detours. And one presented itself as soon as we started to walk down the library steps. "Becky!" Max said urgently. "It's Mr. G!"

"Mr. G? Where?"

"There!" and Max thrust a finger in the direction of the crowd on the sidewalk. "Should we follow him?"

Since I could not think of any very good reason *not* to follow him, there was only one reasonable answer. "Yes, of course! Come on!"

Following James Nassur was no easy trick. That man has long legs! But his speed was not the only problem—it was also approaching rush hour, which means every man for himself as far as the pedestrians of New York are concerned. Dodging harried commuters, returning shoppers, and tired hot-dog vendors, Max and I chased Mr. G, the antelope, up to the corner of 42nd Street and followed him east to Grand Central Station, where he pulled open a door and slipped inside. Then James Nassur fairly skated down the long cement ramp on the other side of the door, somehow neatly avoiding everyone who was struggling up it.

Max, on the other hand, almost charged into a flower seller who had set his tubs of carnations down right in the middle of the ramp—and he did sideswipe one of the tubs, which the carnation man caught just before it rattled down the incline. The man held up a fist full of bedraggled flowers and shook them angrily as we ran on, with the water lapping at our heels.

Mr. G took a fast right off the ramp and then, finally, slowed to a normal pace as he came into a squarish hall in front of the Oyster Bar Restaurant. He seemed to be looking for someone—who turned out to be a little man in an electric blue suit with a maroon-striped tie. "Jonathan!" he said and shook the man's hand. "I thought I was going to miss you." And then Jonathan said something-or-other as they moved into a corner to get out of the way of the people who were heading for the Lower Level. To be safe, Max and I took up position in the corner farthest away, diagonally across the hall.

"What?" Max had just whispered something about the gallery.

"I didn't say anything."

"You must . . . ." and then I heard it again, but Max was looking directly at me and he *wasn't* saying anything.

"At the Two Continents—it will be a nice piece of . . . ."

Trembling, I looked around us. I looked across the hall to where Jonathan and Mr. G were standing, talking quietly. I looked behind us at the rushing commuters, and up at . . . . "My God! Max! It must be a whispering arch!"

"What are you talking . . . ?"

"Shhhh!" I knew that if we could hear their conversation, they could also hear ours. Consequently, it was not the time to explain to Max about whispering arches—arches which carry sound in a way that enables a person standing all the way across a room, at the other side of the arch, to hear a conversation quite distinctly, that he would not have been able to hear at all had he stood in the middle. Unenlightened, but obedient, Max hushed.

Still, it was not the easiest thing in the world to pick up James Nassur's discussion, what with the constant shuffle of footsteps and babble of other voices in the hall. I tilted my head nearer the wall.

Mr. G cleared his throat as Jonathan asked about the current art market in New York City. Mr. G said, "That's a silly question," and laughed. Jonathan snickered too. Then they talked about Jonathan's house in the country and his poodle, Rex. I thought we might already have missed all the good stuff, but I was mistaken.

"Of course, Jon. Why don't you come by tomorrow . . . ?"

". . . I was hoping to go to Broome Street . . . pay an unexpected little call . . . ha, ha."

"Not necessary . . . Wednesday evening at the gallery . . . everyone will be there . . . young man . . . Ha, ha . . . ."

". . . about his black moustache."

"Don't be silly. I saw through the disguise right away. . . ."

"You're a shrewd man, James. . . . He's dealing with the best, I'd say. . . ."

"I'll keep my fingers crossed . . . should be able to hold him . . . . I'm sure they'll make a deal."

"I admire your courage . . . . quite a risk."

"Yes, well, anyway, come by tomorrow and find out . . . . Some very interesting things will be going on—*very* interesting, indeed. Ha, ha . . . ."

Jonathan joined Mr. G in a final malicious chuckle and they shook hands. Then they split up; Jonathan went off in the direction from which he had come, and Mr. G continued on past the Oyster Bar and up another ramp.

Maybe James Nassur realized that we were following him because, a second later, he executed a lightning-like turn and dashed up a flight of steps. So did we—almost. We made the same turn and ran smack into a stream of people coming down. In the excitement, Max lost his footing. I retrieved him at the bottom of the stairs.

167

"Be careful!" I hoisted him to his feet and charged back up the steps.

"I was being careful! I just fell . . . ."

I bounded out at the top of the stairs, into the main concourse. I whirled around, frantically scanning the thousands of faces, but it was too late—James Nassur had slipped away into the rush-hour crowds.

 48

"Becky?" Max asked as we headed for the subway and our ride home—the trip to the Donnell had been quietly forgotten—"Why do you think Mr. G wanted Jonathan to come down to the gallery tomorrow? It's only Tuesday."

"I don't know, but I figure if it's worth Jonathan's time to find out, it just may be worth ours."

"So we're going back?"

"Yes. But that's not the only reason—there was all that stuff about being able 'to hold him' and 'making a deal,' about being able to 'see through his disguise.'"

"Uh-oh. . . ."

"Yeah. That means they know Potter's a double agent and that he's not really working for them."

"What do you think they'll do to him?"

"Max, do you know the meaning of the word *hostage*?"

"Hostage! Gosh! We've got to warn Potter."

"Yes," I said and nodded. "That's exactly what we have to do."

I've never been very good at dialling long-distance calls. I had just finished speaking to Bernie something-or-other in Port Michael, Wisconsin, for the second time.

"Max, are you sure you gave me the right number?"

Max held my mother's little book of numbers in front of my face. "See?"

"All right. Hold it steady." I stuck my finger into the dial and tried again. I could hear the clicking of the machinery, and then the phone on the other end rang. I held my breath.

"Um . . . hello . . . ?" It was not Bernie. It was a very sleepy voice.

"Hello?"

"Hello?"

"Hello! Is Potter Crisply there?"

"Oh. Oh, Potter . . . ah, gee, no . . . he's not," said Potter's "roommate."

"This is his sister. I need to get in touch with him— I *have* to talk to him."

"Well . . . ah, I could have him call you . . . but I don't know when he'll be back. . . . He's away for a few days."

"He's not in Cambridge?"

"No, he's not."

"Great," I said sarcastically. I thought I'd give it one more try. "Listen, this is an emergency—a real live *emergency.*"

"Really?"

"Really!"

"Well, in that case . . . um, there is one number you could try in New York . . . ah, Potter may have gone to see a friend there . . . he had to have his appendix out, all of a sudden—the friend, that is. . . ." (I was beginning to wonder how much this guy was getting paid to do Potter's cover-up for him.)

"What's the number?" I said, cutting him short.

"Oh, that, yeah." He rattled off seven digits.

"Thanks."

"Anytime."

Click. Click.

"You got the Broome Street number?" Max asked incredulously.

"Sure did." I pointed at the piece of paper with my prize and went back to dialling the phone.

"But his note said he wouldn't be back till Wednesday."

170

"It never hurts to try, Max." Sometimes it doesn't help either. Ten rings later: "He's not home."

"That's what I said."

"Well, we'll just have to keep trying him until he is."

"Till Wednesday?"

"If that's how long it takes, yes. He might come back earlier than . . ." I stopped as the front door-bell rang. Since it was Mom's late night and Dad had not yet returned from his office, I figured I was elected to see who it was.

"Yes?" I called through the door and lifted the peep-hole cover—I have my New York door-answering routine almost perfected. I put my eye to the hole—and gasped.

"Eees Meessus Creesply home?"

"N-n-no," and then to Max, "It's X!"

"Ah . . . I zee. Eees Meester Creesply home zen, leetle geerl?"

How could he tell my age through a three-inch-thick door? I tried to sound older. "Not right n-n-now . . . but he will be *soon.*"

"Ah, yez . . . vell zen, I veel be back later. . . . Sank you—sank you very mush."

I do not know exactly what "later" meant to Mr. X, but thankfully, we did not find out. The next doorbell was only my father announcing that he was home.

171

Half an hour later, the three of us sat down to an epicurean feast of Campbell's Tomato Soup and corned-beef hash. When my mother rolled in at her usual Monday hour, we were already washed and ready for bed. Mr. X had not returned.

-------------------→ 49

School is usually a trial, but not nearly as much of one as it was on Tuesday. I tried phoning Potter about thirty times during the day, and when I wasn't trying to *call* him, I was fidgeting in my seat and *thinking* about him—and just waiting for school to end. At the first ding of the last bell, I was out the door and on my way to collect Max. And about thirty minutes after that, the two of us were downtown once again, watching the Two Continents Gallery from our post across the street.

"You can tell something's up," I said and pointed. "They've got two pretzel men on guard today." What was equally impressive was the great pains someone had taken to make the second cart look authentic: it was rusty and dirty and it had old Italian-ice stickers peeling off the side. And today, for a change, the pretzel business was pretty good. Over in the gallery, a number of gents were working up healthy appetites while carting around all shapes and sizes of frames and canvases, hammering continuously, and generally making a terrible racket. It looked as if they were hanging a new show. I wondered what was really going on.

Meanwhile, next door, the good old reliable guys from Ace Radio and TV were, if you can believe it, unloading yet another van of electronic components.

"Why are they doing that?" Max asked.

"Doing what?"

"Doing *that*—they're putting the radio stuff that belongs to the hardware store into the gallery basement. Don't they know they're going down the wrong hatch?"

I looked again. Yes, indeed. Ace Radio and TV was moving boxes into the wrong cellar. "Maybe the gallery's renting out excess storage space . . . ," I began. "Unless . . . unless all that TV and radio equipment is really meant for the gallery in the first place. . . ." And then it hit me like a ton of bricks.

"Of course! Of course, of course, of course—" Max punched me to turn me off. "*Of course*, they're putting those boxes in the gallery basement. Of course, they *have* to put the boxes in the basement—because they're building a *transmitter* in the basement! How could I ever have been dumb enough to think that they needed to go all the way to Thirty-fourth Street! Of course, of course, of course. . . ." I wasn't really trying to be obnoxious; it's just that I'd been waiting for this moment for what seemed like ages—the moment when all the little bits and pieces, all the dribs and drabs of information we had seen and heard and smelled and touched and even tasted (remember the blueberry blintzes?) over the last few weeks would finally fall into place.

"Oh, Max, Max, Max, Max. . . ." I gave him a big hug.

"Becky!" Max shouted in exasperation.

"Shhh! They'll hear you!"

"I'm going to *defect* if you don't tell me what's going on!"

"Oh, dear, lovable, kind, wonderful, thoughtful Max. I'm going to explain it *all* to you—every single thing!"

"Well, it's about time *someone* did."

Max and I moved back around the corner, where we could talk more privately. Then I began. "You see, we were terribly wrong ever to imagine that the Russians were going to take over the Empire State Building."

"We were?"

"Yup. All they had to do was to find out something about its power supply and that, ostensibly, was the information contained in the diagrams Potter delivered. And instead of taking over the building and using the transmission facilities there, all they have to do is cut off the building's power supply, which is a much simpler operation. When the power goes off, it will knock out the building's transmitter and the regular stations will go off the air. Then the Russians can take over broadcasting on those same frequencies, and they can do it from right here—from this innocent-looking gallery—with the mammoth transmitter they've been putting together in the cellar."

"Jeepers!" Max exclaimed.

"Remember that mysterious, padlocked back room with the 'No admittance' sign?"

"Yeah."

"Well, it must be the control room. . . . And that smokestack you were once kind enough to point out isn't a smokestack at all, but a transmission tower."

Max gulped and raised his eyes toward the stack.

"And all the hammering that's going on while they put up the new show is only to cover up the really important noise that's going on downstairs while they assemble the new transmitter."

"Whew!" Max was obviously dazzled by my brilliance.

"But there's more," I continued. "It's about Potter and the diagrams."

"Yeah?"

"Potter was going to set up a trap for the Russians.

175

He was supposed to have Mr. G and the Russians believe that he was on their side and that he was delivering the electrical plans and frequency instructions for the Empire State Building. Once the Russians had the diagrams (they weren't supposed to find out they were fakes) they would go ahead with their scheme for a city-wide disturbance. Okay?"

"Right."

"So the CIA must have figured that when all the key Russian spies assembled here on Wednesday night, they would be able to move in, in a surprise attack, and round up all the Russian agents—remember Potter's note: 'pray for government intervention'? If the CIA were to have carried it off, it probably would have devastated the Russian Intelligence system for years to come."

"Sounds pretty smart to me," Max interjected.

"Yes, it does. But the catch is that Potter has to show up at the gallery on Wednesday evening so the Russians don't suspect it's a trap. Which would have been okay, except that Mr. G figured out that Potter is really working for the CIA. Which means that Nassur knows the diagrams Potter gave him are inaccurate, and therefore, he must have gotten the correct information through other sources. As a result, the Russians really will be able to knock out the ESB transmitter and broadcast on their own. That's problem number one. And problem number two is that when Potter walks in there on Wednesday, he isn't going to be rescued by the CIA as planned because, now that the Russians know who he really is, they intend to use him as a hostage."

"So *that's* where the hostage part comes in."

"Yes, sir. They'll threaten to dispose of Potter unless the CIA stays at a safe distance and allows them to continue their broadcast. And after they're finished, they'll use his release to bargain for their own safe passage out of the country."

"Gosh!" Max sort of whistled through his teeth. "That's awful." I nodded assent. "But, Beck, where does Mr. X fit in?"

"I think that's pretty obvious. Mr. X somehow managed to find out about the Russian broadcast plans, and now Mr. X and the people he works for think they'll cash in. He and his cronies intend to move in on the gallery Wednesday and take over the newly built Russian transmitter so they can broadcast *real* propaganda. They'll let the Russians do all the work and then use it for their own purposes—they're lazy but resourceful."

"But if the CIA and X's friends all move in at the same time . . . ."

"The outcome will depend on who gets there first, but either way—any way—Potter is in *big* trouble."

Max nodded and then added, "But if X knows

and the CIA knows and the Russians know the CIA knows . . . ." I could tell Max was starting on a long string of "buts."

"Listen, Max," I said. "Believe me, everything fits together."

 50

"Take all of it," I said, "we're going to need it."

It wasn't the greatest way to start the morning but Max was down on his hands and knees gathering up the coins from among the broken bits of his bank. Somehow, he had failed to mention the existence of this little cache on Sunday. But now his contribution to the general effort was a matter of necessity. We had a lot to do before 7:30, and today—of all days—we couldn't take a chance on running out of money. Still, Max had looked kind of choked up, and even I had had to wipe a tear from my eye, when he'd brought the hammer down on Popo the Pig's head.

Mom walked into the kitchen; she was in the process of rummaging through everything in her briefcase. "Ah, here it is!" She held up a paper and then, satisfied, shoved it back into the general disarray of her satchel. "By the way, Becky, how come . . . . What's that?" she said suddenly, squinting in our direction.

"What's what?"

"Heavens! It's Popo the Pig!" said my mother, who is good at identifying smithereens.

"It was an accident. He fell."

"He fell down two flights of stairs from Max's bedroom?" She eyed the debris. "And I suppose poor Popo just happened to fall on a hammer—coincidentally?"

"Yes," I said, staring her straight in the eye. After all, it was Max's piggy bank, not hers.

She wisely changed the subject. "Well, I have to run. I have an important date with some early-thirteenth-century manuscripts. See you at six o'clock."

"Right," I said, inadvertently (for a change) adding another lie to my steadily lengthening list.

My mother bent over and kissed us good-bye.

"Good-bye."

"Good-bye."

"Good-bye—be good children."

"Don't worry, we will."

While Max was off brushing his teeth, it occurred to me that we might be able to warn Potter by letting the CIA know the Russians had discovered their plans. I wasn't sure exactly what I'd say, and I was afraid they'd think I was some kind of crank (or worse, some

179

kind of counterspy), but the pros and cons of the matter were quickly settled by looking in the Manhattan phone directory. There was no listing for the Central Intelligence Agency.

As I stashed the White Pages in the cupboard, Max reappeared. It was time to get going. I tried to persuade Max that the best way to carry Popo's treasure might be to dump it in my father's big leather tobacco pouch, but Max insisted on stuffing it all in his pockets. This accomplished a number of things. First of all, it meant that Max was definitely not going to blow away, even in a very strong wind. Second, it proved beyond a shadow of a doubt that a belt is an invaluable piece of equipment. Even so, Max sagged a lot and made a peculiar jingling sound when he walked. I decided it would be prudent to head for the nearest bank and cash Max in. I didn't think truant officers hung out around banks.

"Are you sure we're doing the right thing?"

"In this case, Max, skipping school is not a crime. It's your patriotic duty."

"It is?"

I guided Max into a bank and helped him unload his pockets in front of a teller, while at the same time, saving out a couple of dimes for later. I'd already called Broome Street twice, so Potter was either still "up north," or perhaps, by now, he was out wandering around the streets of New York. "I wish Potter's note had said what time he'd be getting back today."

"Yeah," Max agreed, as he picked through the lint at the bottom of his pockets.

"Would you like fives or tens?" The teller had finished counting.

"Fives or tens?"

"Twenty dollars, in fives or tens?" the man repeated tonelessly.

I'd always known Max was frugal, maybe even stingy, but I never would have guessed that he'd cornered the market in nickels and dimes. I thought back on all the ice-cream cones I'd bought him out of *my* allowance.

"Fives," I said and took the money. Max graciously decided not to argue custody.

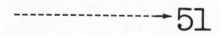 51

"All right. Where do we go from here?" Max looked considerably better—and less lumpy—without ten pounds of change in his pockets.

I looked up at the clouds in the sky. It looked as though it might have been a mistake not to have taken an umbrella with us. "Well," I said, trying to sound very positive, "I thought we'd try looking for Potter in the places we've found him before." And then, hoping to convince myself as much as Max, I added, "There may only be one chance in a million that he'll show up again—but there's always that chance."

"One in seven million, eight hundred ninety-five thousand, five hundred and sixty-three."

"What?"

"One chance in seven million, eight hundred . . . ."

"Thank you. I think we agree that the odds aren't in our favour. But they weren't in our favour any of the other times we spotted him either. Maybe we'll be lucky again."

"Yeah—except he's probably still 'up north.'" Max is a born optimist.

I thought the best procedure would be to begin uptown and then to work our way downtown. Consequently, our starting point was the Central Park Zoo.

The first thing we noticed was that the monkeys were sitting languidly in the bottom of their cage; the most vivacious among them was halfheartedly picking the lice out of a cell-mate's fur. Max quickly set himself the task of cheering them up, and while Max was making a spectacle of himself (though he followed my orders not to make a *noisy spectacle*), I went off to look for Potter.

Searching the zoo turned out to be quite a project—what with almost being trampled by a herd of over-

182

eager kindergartners, and all—but I valiantly made the rounds: reptiles, birds, amphibians, mammals—the whole bunch. Except for the men's room, which I figured I'd just have to take on faith, it was a very thorough inspection—and one that yielded not a single trace of Potter. I guess some people prefer their zoos post meridian.

Finally, I walked back over to the monkey cages to claim Max, who had already made every silly face in the book and laughed himself hoarse. But the monkeys showed no signs of having recovered from their depression, and Max looked near exhaustion. He sank onto a nearby bench.

"How'd you do?"

"Nothing."

"Figures."

"Don't say that. You'll discourage me."

"Well, *I'm* discouraged."

"So, who told you to cheer the monkeys up, anyway?" I have a hard heart where the simian slumps are concerned. "Come on; we've got to be going."

"Roger!" Max stood up, recharged. "Where to?"

"Polk's, folks."

"Right!" Max took a single step. "Beck?"

"Yes?"

"What if Potter shows up here while we're at Polk's Hobbies?"

"Max." It came out as a sort of groan.

"I just thought I'd ask."

"Well, don't—*please*." And I hurried Max out of the zoo.

 52

Since it was before noon, Polk's wasn't exactly jumping either. I ran my hand across an assortment of felt beanie kits and string-it-yourself plastic necklace sets.

"Can I help you?"

"Um, no thanks. I was just looking for someone." Since there was almost no one in the store, I guess that sounded a little suspicious—or else I have a dishonest face and just never noticed—but the salesman evidently assumed that we were up to no good. He started following us, staying exactly five paces behind. I shoved my hands into my pockets and continued the search up and down the aisles. After a few disappointing minutes, we headed for the second floor.

When we got to the top of the stairs, Max, a creature of habit, headed immediately for the models. He began looking through the stacked boxes.

"Max, did it ever occur to you that Potter wouldn't be hiding in among the model airplanes?"

"Sure. Why would he be here? I'm just looking for the Wright Brothers' Biplane—they didn't have one last time I was in."

"Max. . . . Never mind." Between depressed monkeys and the legacy of Kitty Hawk, I was getting precious little help. Resigned, I went off on a tour of the aisles by myself.

When I returned a few minutes later, Potterless, Max was staring into a box of little plastic bits and pieces.

"I think I'll get this one," he said, satisfied.

"Max, not now. We're on *business*." I felt it was about time I reminded him.

"I know, but this is a *very* rare model."

"Max . . ."

"It's not very big."

". . . your brother . . . "

"I promise I'll carry it myself."

". . . is in terrible danger."

"And I won't open it until tomorrow."

"Max . . . ," I sighed.

"Besides, it's my money. . . ."

A few minutes later, Max and I and the Wright Brothers' Biplane, having failed to locate Potter in hobby heaven, set off once more.

-----------------→ 53

"Our timing's not bad," I said.

"Yeah, but if you'd slow down just a little, I could really get in step."

I gave Max one of my what-the-heck-are-you-talk-ing-about looks before I realized that, in spite of the crowds of shoppers on Delancey Street, we were strid-ing along in perfect time with one another, like two renegade Rockettes.

"No, I meant the time of day; it's a good time of day to search a restaurant—it's lunchtime."

Max is not the sort of person who needs to be re-minded about meals. "I know, I'm *famished*!" And so saying, Max took off at double time down Delancey Street.

One of the nice things about places like Ratner's is that they don't change. The plastic flowers can't wilt and the ceiling can't unpink itself. About the only things that move are the people—speaking of which, the host seemed to be temporarily absent. But this was just as well, since it meant that we could simply walk down the aisle and scout around for our missing brother without any interference.

We strolled toward the back, carefully noting customers along the way. When we got to the last row, Max plunked down onto a pink seat.

"Come on, Max."

"Come on where? I can see the door from here."

"Potter's not here. We're going."

"Going!" His tone suggested that I was stark, raving mad. "What about lunch?"

Obviously, old Moneybags Max didn't realize that the conservation of a vast fortune requires careful financial management; so does twenty dollars, plus a couple of dimes, minus one Wright Brothers' Biplane and four subway tokens.

"It will cost us an arm and a leg if we eat here," I said and then, remembering our last visit, "that is, if we *both* eat here."

"No blueberry blintzes?" One addict in the family had been enough.

"Sorry. Some other time."

Reluctantly, Max hoisted himself out of his chair and followed me out the front door.

"I figure we can have a hot dog out here and keep an eye on Ratner's at the same time." Poor Max was too hungry to reply, so he just nodded his head. I found a hot-dog wagon without any difficulty—a pretty normal-looking wagon. In the past week, however, Max had developed a certain caution about vendors and pushcarts. "That guy looks suspicious."

"He looks bored, if you ask me."

"Are you sure he didn't follow us here?"

"Don't be silly—he couldn't climb the subway stairs with a fully loaded hot-dog cart."

Reason always prevails. So does hunger. "All right." Max sauntered over. "I'll take two hot dogs—mustard, ketchup, sauerkraut, pickles—the works."

"Make mine a single, plain, please." I was not quite sure whether Max's order reflected the fact that everything other than the hot dog was free or whether he had suddenly developed a death wish. I soon concluded it wasn't the latter, since he insisted on lifting both bun tops and doing a quick check for foreign objects or, as he put it, "*firecrackers* and stuff!"

Having found nothing too peculiar, Max didn't take long to down his U.S. Grade A, Inspected Inspected hot dogs. Then we settled down to watch Ratner's for twenty-five minutes before the hunger pangs hit again.

"How about some chestnuts?"

"Good idea." I handed him some change and then went off to call Broome Street for the hundredth time. When I returned, Max was cracking chestnut shells. I took a nut.

"Hot!" I yelped and dropped the chestnut into my lap.

"Sure, they're best that way. I had the guy run his

188

blow torch over them a couple of extra times."

I waved my second chestnut around in the air to cool it off. "Did you see anyone interesting go into Ratner's?"

"Uh-uh. Except there was a guy across the street walking his boa constrictor on a leash."

"Max . . . ."

"It's true!"

I was afraid Max was beginning to hallucinate—and I thought that it might be time to move on again. "Well, I don't know about you, but I'm ready to give up on Ratner's."

"Me too," Max answered, jiggling the empty shells in their little brown bag. And while he disposed of same, I went inside to have another quick look around, just in case Potter had slipped past while we weren't looking. But it didn't seem to be our lucky day.

 54

Somehow, some way, and in some order, we managed to cover an incredible amount of ground during the afternoon. Our tortuous path included a return to every other place we could remember having seen

Potter—the Strand Book Store, Surma Book and Music Co., Ferrara's Pastry Shop, Washington Square Park, the Chinatown Book Company, etc., etc. There was still no answer at Potter's; the Two Continents Gallery was all closed up with its blinds drawn; and Clara, the Fortune-Telling Chicken, had nothing to say. As a matter of fact, she even refused to give us our fortune. I wondered if that was an omen.

Finally, we had just a single place left to go. Discouraged, but not defeated, Max and I made our way to Broome Street to wait, we hoped, for Potter's return —and, as if things weren't bad enough already, it began to drizzle.

Many damp minutes later, I looked at my watch. "It's six-thirty, Max."

"Uh-huh."

I sighed sadly. "I guess that means Potter won't be coming back here after all—he'll probably go directly to the gallery now from wherever he is."

Max nodded. "I think you're right."

"So we won't be able to warn him . . . and the Russians will be waiting for him." This was definitely turning into a dismal train of thought. . . . But we still had one tiny, almost infinitesimal ray of hope. "Max—there's only one thing to do."

Max looked up at me. "We're going to get the police?"

190

"The police? No." I stood up and shook the raindrops from my jacket. "We're going to get Mom and Dad."

--------------→ **55**

I'd barely had time to catch my breath on the subway ride uptown, but as soon as the train doors opened, Max and I were off and running again. As we rounded our home corner, the first thing I saw was that the lights in my mother's study weren't on. I prayed that she hadn't chosen this evening to sit around and discuss Chaucer with her Ph.D. candidates, especially since we only had fifty-fifty odds on my father's being home—that's the best you ever get in a doctor's house.

I unlocked the door as quickly as I could with my shaking hands, stepped into the hallway, switched on the light—and almost tripped over Dan, who was sniffing at a piece of paper that was lying in the middle of the floor. Fortunately, Max snatched it out of Dan's drooling jaws before he could devour it. It was a note in my mother's handwriting:

" Dear Becky,

" Welcome home—as you can see, Daddy and I are out. Please make sure you feed Dan and Armenia—and Max. There are TV dinners in the freezer for you and the latter. We won't be late. Sorry I didn't let you know before, but something came up and we had to go downtown. If you need us, we're at the Two Continents. . . . "

"Egad, Max! Come on!" And before the note had even fluttered back to the floor, Max and I had dashed out the door and were running down the sidewalk.

"Popo! Max, wait! We've got to get a cab!" I jumped out into traffic and started flailing my arms wildly, but to no avail. The cars—red, blue, green, but especially yellow—streamed around me and sped away. Oh, if only my mother had let me practise!

Max dashed back and ran into the street. "Becky! You can't!" screamed my little brother, who had come to save me from getting untidy tyre marks down the middle of my nice, new goose-down parka—but instead of dragging me off to safety, Max, in best second-grade fashion, raised his hand. A second later, to my utter astonishment, a shiny yellow cab screeched to a halt.

"Where to, kids?"

"The Two Continents Gallery on West Broadway, and make it snappy—*very* snappy." I sank into the fake leather of the back seat and looked at Max, who was still clutching his biplane. Around us, the buildings merged into a speedy blur as we raced downtown in some wild hope of averting—if that were still possible —a disaster that now threatened to involve not only our intrepid (and beloved) brother, but our well-meaning (and much beloved) parents as well. A head-line flashed through my mind: FIVE CRISPLYS MEET UNTIMELY END TOGETHER: THEY WERE SUCH A NICE FAMILY. What had we ever done to deserve this?

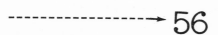 **56**

Our fearless driver, after zooming down Broadway, slammed on the brakes and let us off at Spring Street. With a grateful heart, I handed him the rest of Popo's treasure, and with a grateful heart, he sped away into the night. It had been raining again downtown, and although it had now stopped, everything was soaking —soaking, and dark in spite of the street lights. As quietly as we could, we clomped and squelched our way to the corner and then up West Broadway, toward the gallery.

"It's started, Max!" I could see the people going inside: dark figures silhouetted against the lights that shone through the gallery windows. Also, near the door, I could see two or three men standing motionless—I guessed they were guards and decided that it would be prudent to stay well out of their field of vision. I had no idea how long we had before the plan to sabotage the power for the Empire State Building would go into effect. I could only hope that it would take time to get everyone organized—but of course, I was assuming they hadn't already pulled the plug. In the dim light, I could see that my watch said 7:35.

Since we were approaching from the south, we were able to make our way into the parking lot without crossing in front of the building. I looked around cautiously, but we seemed to be the only ones in the lot, and although it struck me as being awfully careless of Mr. G to have left the side of the building unguarded like that, I was not about to complain. We moved to the wall and our window. There was no car underneath.

"Psssst! Max, the ladder!" We felt our way along the wall toward the rear. Then Max and I scrambled —as nearly as one can scramble on a treacherously wet ladder—up to the roof.

Like everything else around, the roof resembled one big puddle, and to make matters worse, it was even darker up there—pitch black except for a square of light outlining the partly open hatch at the roof's centre, which, when Max leaned over the rim, lit his face with an eerie and unnatural glow. We heard voices below— lots of them.

"There must be a million spies down there," Max whispered.

"Or maybe," I said grimly, "they've caught the whole CIA rescue team."

"Or maybe it's Mr. X and his friends."

"Or . . . Max! Don't—be careful, you'll push it . . . ." And then it went. I held my breath as the Wright Brothers' Biplane slipped through the hatch and vanished into the room below.

Suddenly, downstairs, all was silent. Then the shuffle of feet, and someone saying in a mocking voice, "Relax, it's only a little kid's model airplane!" The babbling of voices resumed.

"I'm sorry!" Max whispered weakly.

"Never mind that now, we've got to get out of here!" And with Max close behind, I scurried back across the roof and down the ladder. But as we stepped to the ground, I became aware of the sound of people talking and running—and I didn't need to listen very long to know that they were running toward the parking lot. I grabbed Max and pulled him back into the dark corner with me, into the shadow of the doorway near the ladder, where we flattened ourselves against the cold steel door. Then, trembling, we listened as the running feet and the angry voices came closer and closer, as men with flashlights directed torch beams from car to car around the lot, as . . . as the knob beside us suddenly turned and the door gave way behind us. . . . Unable to steady myself, unable to stop myself, I fell smack into the waiting arms of James Nassur!

"My, my—we've been expecting you," came the cruel voice, followed by his evil laugh. "Would you like some champagne?"

"Help! Help! Hhhheeeellllpppp!"

"I don't . . . . please, won't . . . oh . . . ." I shook my head. I was trying not to cry—or not to laugh. "Please, won't someone tell us what's going on!" James Nassur put a glass of champagne in my hand. As I looked around the room, I saw that almost everyone else was holding one too—and when I say "everyone," I mean *everyone*: James Nassur, Mom, Dad, Potter, Mr. X, the lady who worked at the gallery, Jonathan, the man from behind the counter at the Strand Bookstore and a ton of people I'd never even seen before . . . everyone!

"Please," I moaned, my head spinning.

My mother patted me gently on the shoulder, while my father, who was holding a broken wing piece from Max's biplane, kept looking at the hatch and shaking his head. "It's all right, dear," she soothed. "There's a good explanation for everything," and then added, "It's just that we haven't gotten one yet. Right now, though, I wish you'd explain to me how Max and . . . ."

"Becky!" Potter, who had just loped across the room, cut her short. He was smiling broadly. "It's a gallery opening!"

"Of course," James Nassur seconded. "It's the opening of a show of works by a very talented young artist named Winston Potter Crisply." He held his champagne glass up for a toast.

"It's a party!" Jonathan bubbled.

"And a family reunion," observed my mother.

"It's a surprise," remarked my father.

"Boy! You can sure say that again!"

Transmitter? Russians? Spies?

The walls mocked me. Well, not the walls exactly, but what was on them; they were covered with Potter's "diagrams," which had been mounted in neat new plexiglas frames and hung around the room.

Potter followed my gaze. "Do you like them? I call the technique 'Nouveau Collage.'" He motioned toward a certain specimen, which just happened to have a picture of the Empire State Building glued down in one corner.

"That's art?" asked Max, who was becoming a little brash—what with the glass of champagne he'd just downed and all. I gave him a stern look.

"Not bad," I said.

"Well, I just *love* them," announced a lady in a long black gown, as she floated past.

The "diagrams" weren't the only things on the walls, though. There were paintings that I'd never seen before.

"The colours are sensational, aren't they?" said my father, who was standing nearby.

"That's art?" Max repeated. He was weaving a little from side to side.

I poked him. "It sure beats Alfred Ornstickler."

Max bobbed his head up and down in agreement.

"Actually," I said, the soul of magnanimity, "they're kind of nice."

Potter beamed. A dark-suited man turned to join the discussion. "Ah," he said and gestured at one of the larger canvases. "Notice the subtle tonalities, the pleasing use of light and shadow—the manner in which the feathery quality of the brushwork hints at an ethereal and transcendent presence. I'd say that the aesthetic variables have been handled with consummate skill."

"Thank you," said Potter, modestly.

The gentleman bowed, clicked his heels together, and removed the monocle from his eye. "Well, if you'll excuse me, I think I'll go find another glass of champagne. It's very good—even if it does come from New York State." And then he headed off for the refreshment table.

"Who was *that*?" I asked. "*Weird.*"

"Oh, him? He's one of the 'cutthroats.' . . ." Potter looked slightly embarrassed and glanced around to see if anyone had heard him. "I mean," he said more cautiously, "he's one of the critics. They don't usually show up at openings. I guess he made an exception."

"I wonder why."

"Yeah, why?" said Max, suddenly rejoining the conversation.

"Why? I suppose he had nothing better to do to-night."

"No," said Max stubbornly. "I mean *why?*"

Potter, who thought he'd just given a simple answer to a simple question, gave Max a quizzical look. But Max was not after simple answers. And I had to admit, a thorough explanation did seem to be in order.

"I think," I said, "that he means 'why' with a capital W—Why have you been doing all these strange things?" My voice was a trifle loud. And my parents, who sensed that something interesting was going on, turned around to listen.

"That's not a bad question," said my father.

"Could you narrow it down a little?" asked Potter and smoothed out the folds in his cape.

"All right," I said. "Let's start at the beginning. . . ."

"Good place," said my mother. They all nodded in agreement.

I gathered that I'd been elected family inquisitor. "Okay. Why didn't you tell anyone you were an artist? Why didn't you tell anyone you were living in New York City?"

"How long *has* he been living in New York?" asked my mother.

"Since September," answered Max, "at least."

My mother whistled in amazement, and my father started counting on his fingers and mumbling something about "that's a lot of tuition."

"Well," Potter said and cleared his throat. "I've been drawing for years, although I never told anyone about it—I guess I was sort of embarrassed—and back then it didn't matter because I didn't think of myself as a 'serious' artist. But Harvard changed all that: I saw there were other things a guy could do in life besides having the career in medicine I'd always planned on. And last September, after I'd finished two years pre-med, I came to the conclusion that I wanted—really and truly wanted—to be an artist. So I dropped out and, since New York City is the artistic capital of the nation, I came here to work. But even though I'd made the decision not to become a doctor, I couldn't tell you." He looked at Mom and Dad. "I just couldn't, not after all those years. I figured it would break your heart, Dad—you wanted so much for me to follow in your footsteps."

"But, as everyone can see," said my father, "it's still ticking. Besides, one doctor in the family is too much."

"Yeah," Potter agreed. "I can see all that now—but I didn't know it *then*. And once you start covering up, it's pretty hard to stop. Actually, that part was fun— we didn't do a bad job, did we?"

"Not bad. But you did write all those letters in New York and then ship them back to Cambridge so they could be postmarked properly?"

"Yes," said Potter. He smiled.

"And you did call twice on Mondays to get double

the money you would usually have gotten?" My mother raised an eyebrow on that one. "And you did have someone else go to your classes for you?"

"Yeah. He carried it off pretty well too."

"Except the B's. They were the giveaway," I said.

It was my father's turn. "Say, do you mind telling me whose education we *have* been paying for?"

"Ah . . . that's all been worked out, Dad. But can I talk to you about it later?"

My father began tugging at his ear in a nervous sort of way.

I thought I'd better change the subject. "You would've had to tell us about everything sometime," I pointed out. "At least you could have invited us to the gallery opening—I mean, you are *our* brother and *their* kid."

"Yeah! That's the least you could have done!" said Max. Someone had handed him another glass of champagne.

"Well, yes. Except that at first, I didn't want to tell anyone about my art—*especially* my family—until I was a success: until after the opening, if it went well. But I also knew that the opening could be a terrible fiasco. So I kept everything about it top secret. It was really a matter of pride; I'd be good—and do a really bang-up job—or I wouldn't let anyone know."

I was beginning to hear echoes of Russian Intelligence.

"I changed my mind, though. I decided I wanted you all here."

"But you still didn't tell us," I reminded him.

"By then, I didn't need to—you and Max had been following me all over the city for weeks . . ."

"You knew!"

". . . and I assumed you'd figured everything out."

"Well, almost everything," I said judiciously.

"So I reasoned that, sooner or later, you'd get here —it just turned out to be a little later, that's all. And as for *them*," Potter was pointing an accusing finger at Mom and Dad, "they'd hired *him!*"

We all turned toward Mr. X, who, seeing that he was the centre of attention, grinned sheepishly and waved from the shadows.

"You *did?*" I couldn't believe it.

"We got a little suspicious too," said my mother.

"But we almost didn't get here," my father added. "He didn't figure out until this afternoon that the opening was tonight."

"That will teach you to hire a private eye from the Yellow Pages," my mother sneered.

"It wasn't *my* fault. His ad said 'twenty years experience, better than Dick Tracy' . . . oh, never mind."

"He's got a gun," said Max.

"Pure window dressing," answered my mother. "It isn't loaded."

"And he stood around and mumbled curses . . . ."

"Bunions."

"Huh?"

"Sore feet."

"Aha!" I said. "The squeaky shoes . . . of course!"

"Is he really Dick Tracy?" asked Max.

"Drink your champagne, dear."

"Well, I'm glad everyone got here," said Potter, "in spite of it all."

"And it doesn't look as though you needed to have worried about being a success, either," my father said and put his arm around Potter's shoulders. He looked at the room full of people and beamed.

"At least the preliminary indications are good," Potter agreed. "But in any case, I won't be your problem any more—financially, that is."

"No more double calls on Monday?" asked my mother sardonically.

"No more double calls. It looks like I'll be able to support myself from now on. That man over there," he pointed out a man in grey pinstripes, "wants to make a deal to buy *four* canvases. Mr. Nassur thinks he'll be able to hold him to a good price. I have some other offers too."

"Congratulations." I shook his hand.

"Thanks, but that's not all. Even if the deal falls through, I've always got this—from good old Uncle

Sam." Potter pulled an envelope out of his pocket and waved it around. "It's a government grant—a working grant from the U.S. Arts Foundation—so either way, I'll have enough to live on. It came through today."

"Government intervention?"

"Yeah, you could call it that."

"Thanks," I said, "but I don't believe I invented the term."

"It's wonderful," said my mother. "Absolutely wonderful. And I propose a toast . . . ." She stopped and turned her glass upside down to find that, as she'd suspected, it was empty.

"I'll get some more," my father said and started for the buffet.

"Why don't we all go over?" Potter said. "There are some people I'd like you to meet." So saying, Potter led us through the crowd, gathering a bouquet of flowery compliments along the way.

"Mom, Dad, Rebecca, Max—I'd like you to meet Jonathan Spinkleman."

Jonathan, in an electric green suit, smiled warmly. "How do you do," he said and shook hands with Mom and Dad.

"Jonathan," Potter said, "is the man largely responsible for my being here tonight. He was my art history professor, first semester, at Harvard. And it was he who showed me the light."

Jonathan grinned and lowered his eyes modestly. "Really, I just gave the lad a little advice—when I saw that he had such talent . . . and such enthusiasm. . . ."

"More than that," corrected Potter. "You gave me lots of encouragement, and when I came to New York, you told me who to get in touch with. You even sent me to the Two Continents Gallery, although," Potter chided, "you never told me that you knew Mr. Nassur personally—I didn't find out until tonight that he was your best friend."

"I thought you mightn't come if you knew—young people nowadays are so sensitive about making it on their own. But," Jonathan continued, "I sent you here because he is the best, not because he is my friend. He has more courage than most dealers; it's quite a risk to hang a show by a complete unknown. James Nassur . . . ."

At the sound of his name, the great James Nassur turned around and joined the group. I still couldn't look at him without feeling a sense of dread.

"Mom and Dad, I'd like you to meet James Nassur."

The former Mr. G bowed slightly. "I'm very pleased to make your acquaintance." He looked down at Max and me. "And yours—again."

Max held out his hand. "Are you Russian?" I guess he wanted to salvage some tiny bit of all our hard work.

206

"Russian? Me? No. I'm quite American—I was born here. But my parents were Portuguese, if that's any help."

"No," said Max, "it isn't. It isn't at all."

In due course, we were introduced to at least half the people in the room: Mr. Nassur's secretary, who spoke Hungarian; Mr. X, who had clammy hands and whose real name was Mr. Ree (I think he'd changed it, for professional reasons); Frank, from the Strand; and Sammy, from the Chinatown Book Company. . . . By the time we had reached the other side of the room, I had shaken enough hands to qualify for the presidency.

My mother, who is an old hand at hand-shaking, was worrying about other things. She tilted her champagne glass upside down again to remind Potter that he still hadn't gotten her a refill. Max did the same.

"Wait a minute," I said to Potter. "Before you disappear, there are just a few more small matters I'd like you to clear up."

"Okay. Shoot."

"What happened to your moustache?"

"I took it off."

I couldn't tell whether or not he was being purposely obtuse. I thought I'd try another tack. "Why did you use to wear a fake moustache when you came to the gallery?"

"To look older. I didn't think James Nassur would

take me seriously if he knew I was only nineteen; I thought he'd refuse to take my work."

"But he knew."

"Yeah, I guess so. It was a pretty cheap moustache." Potter pulled a rumpled piece of fuzz out of his pocket and pressed it against his lip. Only one side stuck.

"And the clothes? The big black hat, the cloak?"

My mother eyed his cape. "Yes, isn't that costume a little eccentric?"

"Well, artists *are*, you know. We're allowed." He swished his cape self-righteously.

"Okay," I said. "But what about all that Russian stuff—Russian books, Russian Easter eggs—all of that?"

"Oh, *that*. There was a terrific show of Russian icons here, at the gallery, just a little while ago—it was really good. After that, I got kind of interested in a lot of Russian arts. Like those Easter eggs: it's an old craft for dyeing eggs called Pysanki. . . ."

"Raw?"

"Sure—it's the only way. I'll teach you sometime."

"Thanks." I hardly needed to ask the next question, but I didn't want to leave any stone unturned. "What about all those things you said? What about the 'jungle out there,' and 'standing the world on its ear'; what about a 'real blast,' and 'the high stakes' . . . ?"

"Tsk, tsk, tsk," said Potter. "You really shouldn't listen at keyholes. . . ."

"If I may interrupt," said my father, "I think the answer is that your brother is well-schooled in theatrical lingo."

"Bingo," said Max.

"Slang," said my mother, calling a spade a spade.

"Bang!" said Max.

My father looked at his youngest. "I think it's about time to put something in Max's stomach besides the champagne." He nodded toward the buffet. "Do you suppose there's anything to *eat* over there?"

"Pang!" said Max, getting the idea.

"Sure," said Potter, "follow me."

"I'm *starved!*" Max announced as we neared the table—either he was beginning to sober up, or the proximity of food had brought on temporary lucidity.

"What will it be?" Potter asked, holding five small plates and waving his hand over a table laden with miniaturized food: cocktail franks, little meatballs, baby quiches. . . . Max was carefully walking from one end of the table to the other, sniffing. "How about some of these?" Potter asked and pointed to a tray of tiny sandwiches. "Or these?" he said, indicating a platter filled with crisp, bite-sized dough envelopes, neatly arranged around a bowl of sour cream . . . .

"Blueberry blintzes!"

"Little blueberry blintzes," corrected my mother.

"Blueberry blintzes? Did someone say 'blueberry

blintzes'?" Max hurried back around the table.

"Ah," sighed my father. "Blueberry blintzes."

"Of course," said Potter. "What did you expect?"

 59

I hope that everyone else in the room had had theirs, because, after Potter finished loading our five plates, I'm afraid there weren't many left. But as Potter said, "Etiquette has its place—and it has nothing to do with blueberry blintzes." Anyway, plates laden, we five Crisplys retreated to the quieter side of the room—although with all the "oohs" and "aahs" and "don't-you-just-love-its" that were still going on, things were not exactly silent.

"Well," my mother announced as she eased herself onto a chair, "I'm glad *I* came." And then, remembering the circumstances, she added, "but next time, you'll have to invite me."

"Boy, I'm sure glad *I* came," Max said as he picked up a blintz and smeared the sour cream around the rim of his plate.

"So am I," said my father. "I'm very proud of my

210

artist son. As a matter of fact, I can't think of a more perfect way to have gotten the family together."

"Gee," I said, "I can think of a *few* things *I* wouldn't want to repeat about it. Next time, I could do without the Russian spies, the coded Easter eggs, locked back rooms, fortune-telling chickens, lethal Frisbee throwers in Washington Square Park, suspicious chestnut vendors, TV towers in smokestacks, transmitters in the basement, disrupted trade talks, fishy *New York Times*, double agents, double entendres, triple agents . . . ."

"Quadruple agents," said Max.

Potter laughed. "Well, Becky, let it be a lesson to you."

"What about me?"

"You too, Max. There's a moral in this—somewhere." He paused a minute and then cleared his throat. "You should *both* remember that things are sometimes what they seem." He scratched his head. "I mean, what they don't seem . . . ."

"Things are seldom what they seem," corrected my mother.

"Or what they don't seem," added Max.

"What I'm trying to say," said Potter, "is that things are often just as they appear to be. For instance, I dressed like an artist and went to a gallery—and I really was an . . . ."

"Wrong," I said. "You dressed like a spy and did a bunch of weird things."

"It was all in how you looked at it—which, in your case, was incorrectly. . . ."

"Correctly," I protested, "considering that we were misled."

Potter persisted. "Becky, the point is that sometimes, you should take things at face value, without looking for a deeper meaning."

"Then again, sometimes you shouldn't," said my mother.

"Then again, you hardly ever know which," added my father.

"And sometimes you should stay out of things altogether."

"But sometimes, you can't help falling in. . . ."

"Please!" Potter held up his hand for silence. "All I'm trying to say is that . . . oh, never mind." He smiled and kissed me on the cheek. "I give up."

"I wholeheartedly agree," said Max and swallowed another blueberry blintz.